A Guiding Promise

Gail Chianese

Annie's®

Books in The Inn at Magnolia Harbor series

Where Hope Blooms
Safe Harbor
Binding Vows
Tender Melody
At Summer's End
Mending the Past
Kindred Blessings
Grateful Hearts
Christmas Gifts
Joyful Beginnings
Love's Surprise
Season of Renewal
Drawing Hope
A Guiding Promise
Cherished Legacy
Garden of Secrets
Sweet Wishes
August Retreat
A New Path
Autumn's Spell
Treasured Harvest
Comfort and Joy
A Time to Celebrate
Forever Starts Today

A Guiding Promise
Copyright © 2020, 2025 Annie's.

All rights reserved. No part of this publication may be reproduced, stored in a retrieval system, or transmitted in any form or by any means—electronic, mechanical, photocopying, recording or otherwise—without the prior written permission of the publisher. The only exception is brief quotations in printed reviews. For information address Annie's, 306 East Parr Road, Berne, Indiana 46711-1138.

The characters and events in this book are fictional, and any resemblance to actual persons or events is coincidental.

Library of Congress-in-Publication Data
A Guiding Promise / by Gail Chianese
p. cm.
ISBN: 979-8-89253-229-7
I. Title
2020938316

The Inn at Magnolia Harbor™
Series Creator: Shari Lohner
Editor: Lorie Jones
Cover Illustrator: Bonnie Leick

10 11 12 13 14 | Printed in China | 9 8 7 6 5 4

Grace

"Come on. Give already." Grace Porter gave the nut a couple of smacks with the wrench. She knew it wouldn't actually accomplish anything, but it relieved a little of her stress. Trying to unclog the drain in the kitchen sink was frustrating to say the least.

Grace and her younger sister, Charlotte Wylde, owned and operated the Magnolia Harbor Inn in South Carolina. The two of them made a good team, and Grace loved working with her sister. In the years since they had opened the inn, Grace had learned how to repair most items around the place, which was why she was tackling the drain.

"Not going well?" Charlotte asked.

"No," Grace said. "I guess I should have eaten my spinach at breakfast. Maybe then I'd have enough strength to turn this nut."

Winston, her rescued shih tzu mix, plopped down on the floor and sighed.

Charlotte kneeled down to peek under the sink, as if that would help. "You could call Spencer and ask him to come take a whack at it." She grinned at her own joke.

Little flutters set off inside Grace at the thought of their neighbor Spencer Lewis. Over the past year, their friendship had deepened, and there was something special there, something she wasn't quite ready to name yet.

Charlotte was right. Grace could call Spencer, who would probably drop everything and have the drain unclogged and put back together in no time at all. But she'd been on her own for more than twenty years—too long to lean on a man, even if it made her life easier.

Grace tried again and smiled when the stubborn nut moved a fraction of a centimeter. "No, I've got this. Besides, Spencer's in D.C. for a friend's retirement from the bureau." Spencer was a retired intelligence analyst for the FBI.

Charlotte frowned. "I'm surprised he didn't ask you to go with him."

"Why would he do that?" Grace asked. "We're just friends."

"Are you still singing that tired old song? You can't tell me that all you feel for Spencer is friendship," Charlotte protested. "I've seen the way he looks at you, how he watches you when he thinks no one else notices. He's crazy about you."

"We've only been on a few dates," Grace reminded her. "Why would I go to D.C. with him?"

"To spend time together without the responsibilities of work getting in the way," Charlotte said. "And to give the attraction between you a chance to spark into a fire."

"It's too soon for something like that," Grace said. "When the time is right, it'll be right."

"Yeah, I know. Patience." Charlotte's voice softened, filled with sisterly love. "I only want you to be happy. Hank's been gone a long time, and Jake's grown up. There's no reason for you not to move on."

Grace set the wrench down and thought about Charlotte's words. She tried not to dwell on the past and her tragic, short-lived marriage. She had loved Hank with all her heart. Had it not been for that fatal train accident, she was sure they'd still have a wonderful marriage. But neither Hank nor their son, Jake, was what held her back. She was ready to find someone to spend her life with, and Spencer might be the one, but she didn't want to rush their relationship.

"I am happy," Grace said. "If it's meant to be between us, then it'll happen. In the meantime, I have a drain to unclog, and we have a houseful of guests arriving soon." She returned to cranking away at the nut.

"Fine," Charlotte said. "I understand."

"Speaking of our guests, what time is it?" Determined to win the battle of the clogged drain, Grace was delighted when the nut gave a little more.

"It's one thirty."

"Our first guest is due to arrive any minute. I need to get this drain fixed, and we still have to make up the beds." Grace started to inch out from under the kitchen sink.

Charlotte put her hand on her arm to stop her. "Relax. Winnie said she'll bring over the sheets as soon as they're dry and help me with the beds. The rest of the rooms are spotless and ready to go. I'm going to double-check now." She grinned. "You keep flexing those muscles, and focus on the drain."

Grace thanked her sister and went back to work on the stubborn plumbing. Between the two of them and their aunt, Winnie Bennett, they'd get everything shipshape before the new guests arrived.

On frustrating days, her mother had often said, "What can go wrong will go wrong and always at the worst possible moment." Well, she hadn't been kidding. In the last twenty-four hours, Grace had nearly been in an accident while driving home from the market, the kitchen sink had backed up, and the dryer had gone out.

And of course, they had a full house of guests for the week.

She didn't have time for any more calamities.

There were guests to welcome and chores to finish. If all went well, her reward would be a quiet evening reading before the fireplace with Winston curled up on her lap.

After one more heave at the wrench, the nut came loose. Grace quickly unscrewed it and pulled the trap free, only to get a face full of water. She sputtered and shot up, hitting her head on the cabinet. Grabbing a bucket, she shoved it under the draining pipe as she tried to decide if she should laugh or cry.

"Good morning," Winnie said as she walked into the room. She stopped short, her eyes going wide as she took in the scene. Then a smile tugged at her mouth. "Oh no. Are you all right?"

Grace glanced down at her wet shirt and spread her hands out. "I'm quite a mess, but I'll live."

Winnie laughed and handed her a towel. "That's good to hear. Charlotte wanted me to tell you that Lucinda Grayson called and she's about thirty minutes away."

Grace paused in wiping off her face. "Is her room ready?"

"We've put our best foot forward," Winnie answered brightly.

Grace laughed. "Have you been watching *Mary Poppins* again?"

"You know me," Winnie said, a twinkle in her eye. "I love Julie Andrews."

"I'd better get a move on so I can greet Lucinda," Grace remarked, finishing up.

"I'll make a pitcher of sweet tea," Winnie offered. "I brought over some cookies for your hospitality hour. If I left them at home, your uncle Gus would polish them off within the hour."

"Thank you." For a second Grace thought about kissing her aunt's cheek until she remembered that she was covered with water. She was so blessed to have Winnie in her life. When Grace's mother died several years ago, it was Winnie who got the family through their loss.

Grace showered and dressed, then added a swipe of mascara and a light shade of pink to her lips. She didn't bother drying her hair.

Instead, she ran her fingers through it, knowing the waves she'd been blessed with would do better left on their own.

Winston barked to signal they had company.

Grace wasn't worried about her little dog scaring the guests. She knew he was sitting on the porch with his tail wagging, waiting for attention.

She strode to the front door and opened it. Sure enough, Winston was making friends with their new arrival already.

"Welcome to the Magnolia Harbor Inn. I'm Grace Porter, one of the owners." She smiled at the woman and held out her hand when her guest finished petting Winston. "And I see you've met Winston. He loves visitors."

"What a delightful welcoming party." She shook Grace's hand and glanced around with a serene smile. "I'm Lucinda Grayson. This place is even lovelier than I imagined."

"Thank you," Grace said. "Please come inside, and I'll check you in. You must be tired after driving all the way from Nashville."

Lucinda entered the foyer and followed Grace to the reception desk. "I'm used to getting up early because I have a small farm outside the city. No matter how many times I tell that rooster to let me sleep in, he ignores me." She smiled. "Thankfully, I'm at an age where I'm expected to nap in the afternoon."

Grace laughed. If all their visitors were as sweet and funny as Lucinda, it would be a good week indeed. "While you're a guest here, I promise we'll let you sleep as late as you'd like."

"What a treat," Lucinda said.

Winnie entered the room and introduced herself to Lucinda. "I hope you enjoy your stay."

"Thank you," Lucinda said. "I'm sure I will."

"You'll be in the Bluebell Suite, which has a partial view of

Lake Haven," Grace said. "Your room has a soaking tub. It shares a bathroom with another suite, but we're not expecting that guest until tomorrow."

"It sounds wonderful, especially the tub," Lucinda said.

"We provide wine, cheese, and hors d'oeuvres every night from six to seven on the back veranda," Grace continued. "And breakfast is served in the dining room. If there's anything we can do to make your stay better, please let us know."

"You'll find I'm very low-maintenance," Lucinda said. "I simply want some peace and quiet without someone telling me what to do."

Grace wasn't sure how to respond. Clearly something was going on with her guest, but it was none of her business. "Let me show you to your room." She took Lucinda's luggage and led her upstairs.

Winston trotted after them.

After leaving Lucinda to get settled in, Grace returned to the reception desk with Winston on her heels.

A few minutes later, she heard the sound of car doors slamming outside.

Winston ran to Grace's side and sat beside her, his tail swishing back and forth across the floor.

Grace smiled at the dog. "You're such a gentleman."

The bell above the door jingled, and two couples entered the inn.

"Welcome to the Magnolia Harbor Inn. I'm Grace Porter, one of the owners. If you'll give me a moment, I'll get you all checked in."

Winston made a beeline for the new arrivals and greeted them with a doggy smile.

"That's Winston," Grace said. "He enjoys making friends."

"He's adorable," one of the women gushed as she leaned down to pet Winston. She was in her midforties and resembled a model with her sleek curls and flawless complexion.

The man next to her was in his late forties with smooth, dark skin and short black hair. He approached the desk. "We're Monty and Jamie Robinson."

Jamie joined them and handed Grace a printed e-mail confirmation.

"Thank you," Grace said, scanning the confirmation. "You're here to see your son graduate from Charleston Southern University, if I remember correctly."

"We are." Jamie beamed proudly.

"I graduated from CSU too," the other woman chimed in. She appeared to be in her twenties. "It's a wonderful school. What's your son's major?"

"Music therapy," Monty said.

"That's a great program. My younger brother works with a music therapist for his anxiety." The man with her held out his hand. "I'm Joel Benson, and this is my wife, Felicity."

"We're on our honeymoon," Felicity added, smiling lovingly at her husband.

"Congratulations." Grace smiled. There was nothing as sweet as young love. She turned back to the Robinsons to finish checking them in.

Winston was running around, sniffing all the new arrivals and giving out doggy kisses. Grace was thankful that her dog kept the Bensons entertained while she completed the paperwork.

"The university is about an hour away, but on graduation day, you'll want to allow a little extra time for traffic and parking," Grace advised. "Otherwise, it's an easy and beautiful drive." She handed Monty two sets of room keys.

"The traffic can't be half as bad as Baltimore on a regular day," Monty replied.

Grace chuckled. "That's probably true. If there's anything we can do to improve your stay, please don't hesitate to let us know." She filled the group in on breakfast as well as the evening hospitality hour and made several local restaurant recommendations, including The Tidewater located across the lake. Charlotte's boyfriend, Dean Bradley, was the chef and owner.

Charlotte and Winnie entered the room and warmly greeted the guests.

"Would you mind showing Monty and Jamie to the Buttercup Suite, please?" Grace asked her aunt.

"My pleasure," Winnie said. "You're going to love your room. It has a full lake view and French doors that open to the veranda. Watching the sun rise over the lake is a lovely way to start your day."

"It sounds great," Jamie said.

Winnie ushered the couple up the stairs.

Grace turned her attention to the younger couple, although Felicity seemed more interested in playing with Winston. "We've put you in the Dogwood Suite. It has a king-size bed, a private bath, and a full view of the lake. There are also French doors that open onto the veranda and a fireplace. South Carolina doesn't get particularly cold in May, but it does add a nice ambience in the evenings."

"The room sounds perfect," Felicity said. "I understand you also have rowboats and canoes we can use."

"Yes, we do. But I wouldn't advise swimming in the lake. It's still on the chilly side." Grace filled out the paperwork, then handed them their room keys. "Now, let's get you to your suite so you can start your vacation."

"I'll show them their room," Charlotte offered. As she led them toward the stairs, she told Joel and Felicity about some of the shops in historic downtown Magnolia Harbor. "The Book Cottage carries a wide selection of books and art supplies. Miss Millie's dress shop offers all the latest styles. If you're interested in knitting or quilting, then stop by Spool & Thread."

"I can't wait to check them out," Felicity said.

Grace really appreciated her sister and Winnie helping with the guests. It gave her a few minutes to start her to-do list. She loved the inn, but it came with a never-ending list of chores.

At the top of the list was fixing the dryer, now that she'd cleared the clog in the kitchen drain. She added a reminder to deadhead the strange but pretty pink-flowered bush that was already losing its buds. Then there were the errands for the church fundraiser.

Grace stopped writing and glanced around. She had the oddest sensation that something was coming her way. It didn't make sense. She couldn't ask for a better life. Working with Charlotte was a dream come true. Jake loved his job and kept in touch well. Winnie was a blessing to all around her. And then there was Spencer.

Brushing the odd feeling away, Grace returned to her list. There was no sense in borrowing trouble.

By the time she was done with the list, it was a page long. She laughed and shook her head. "One way or another, I'll get it all done."

Winston suddenly ran to the front door and barked.

A second later, the doorbell rang.

As Grace walked to the door, she wondered why her newest arrival had pressed the bell during the day. She scratched Winston behind the ears, then opened the door.

The man standing there seemed vaguely familiar, but the only guest left to check in today was Gustav Heinz, and she was sure she'd remember someone with that name.

"Welcome to the Magnolia Harbor Inn. I'm Grace Porter, one of the owners." She stepped back and opened the door wider. "Please come inside."

The man smiled but didn't move.

Grace studied him. She was sure they'd met before. His eyes

were familiar. She heard Winnie and Charlotte coming down the stairs. Maybe one of them would recognize him and save her from further embarrassment.

The man's smile faded. He glanced down, and when he met her gaze again, his expression was sad and resigned. "Hi, Gracie."

Only one person had ever called her that nickname. She knew that voice, the timbre and the cadence. She heard it every time she talked to her son.

Their son.

Long-buried memories exploded in her head. Joyful times and stolen moments that marked some of the best and most important days of her life as well as the worst. She stared into his eyes. Eyes she never thought she'd see again. It couldn't be. He was supposed to be dead, which was why it had taken her so long to recognize him.

But how?

Grace grabbed for the door as the room began to spin and the world faded.

"Are you okay?" he asked, his eyes filled with concern.

"Hank?" Grace asked.

"Oh, sweet heavens!" Winnie cried out behind her.

Grace spun around to see her aunt faint at the foot of the stairs. Fortunately, Charlotte caught Winnie. "I've got you," she said gently. She helped Winnie into a chair, then gaped at the man at the door.

Grace hurried over to her aunt, more concerned with the living than the apparition before her.

"She'll be okay. She just had a shock," Charlotte said, not taking her eyes off the man. "Is that really Hank?"

"It can't be him," Grace said, her mind reeling. "This is a dream or a hoax."

She struggled to make sense of the situation, but it was no good. If it was a dream, she wanted to wake up right now. But this didn't seem like a dream. Never in a dream had she felt the solid front door under her hands. So that ruled out one option. But why would someone play such a cruel trick on her, especially after so many years?

Winston growled and charged the man. He tore at his pant leg and attempted to drag him out the door. When the man didn't budge, Winston let go and ran around in front of him. The dog barked and growled, snapping his little teeth.

The man backed up slowly until he was out the door.

Grace stared at her sister. Charlotte's eyes were glazed and wide, her jaw slack, and Grace knew exactly how she felt. Out of life's curveballs, this one had to take the prize.

Winnie came to and slowly straightened. She patted her hair and glanced around. "Did I faint? I could swear I just saw—"

"Hank Porter," Grace said, cutting her off. She marched to the door and peered outside to see him standing at the bottom of the steps. "It appears my dead husband has returned from the grave."

Grace

Charlotte and Winnie both gasped as they joined Grace in the doorway.

"B-but that's impossible," Winnie stammered. "That man can't be Hank."

Grace nodded as she scrutinized the man. If this was a prank, she was impressed, because he looked exactly like Hank. He even stood like Hank. From a distance, the tall and lanky man before her could have passed for her son. She had gazed into those green eyes when they'd exchanged vows. On that special day, his eyes had been so full of light and love.

With a few exceptions—his dark hair was shorter with some gray streaks, and there were a few lines around his eyes—he didn't appear to have aged or changed. How was that possible?

Then Grace noticed one thing that was different about him. A scar ran from the middle of his forehead to his temple and disappeared. Was it from the train accident?

Winston planted himself in front of the women, emitting a deep growl from his little body. It was clear that he considered himself a mighty warrior protecting his family.

"Aunt Winnie, I'm sorry to have given you such a fright," the man said. "Are you all right?"

"I'm not sure since I'm talking to a ghost," Winnie replied.

A small smile flashed across his face. "I can understand the shock you all must be experiencing right now, but I can assure you that I am very much alive."

"That can't be true," Charlotte whispered to Grace. "They identified the body, didn't they?"

"No, they were never able to identify all the bodies on the train," Grace replied. "There was too much damage. Based on the evidence, they presumed Hank was one of them."

"If you'll let me inside, I can explain." Hank took a step forward but stopped when Winston growled at him again.

Grace scooped up her dog and calmed him. "Normally, he's very sweet."

When voices sounded in the foyer, Grace was reminded of the guests. She was thankful they'd been upstairs in their rooms and hadn't observed Hank's arrival. She couldn't imagine what they would think of her or the inn if they had witnessed the scene.

Grace handed Charlotte the dog and whispered, "If you don't mind, I think it's best if Hank and I talk somewhere private. Can we use your cottage?"

"Of course," Charlotte said.

"Thank you," Grace said. "You'd better put Winston in my quarters for now."

"Maybe you should keep him with you," Winnie suggested. "For support and comfort."

"I'll be fine, but I'm so glad you're both here." Grace wanted to keep her sister and her aunt by her side, but they had guests to tend to and an inn to run. Besides, she had a feeling Hank would be more open and relaxed with just the two of them.

Grace led her husband—oh, how weird that sounded—around the inn and down the path to Charlotte's cottage. As they walked, a million questions raced through her mind. She'd save them for when they got inside, but the loudest question was how she was going to tell Jake. Their son had been only a toddler when Hank had died. Now Jake was almost the same age as Hank had been when he'd disappeared. The whole thing was mind-boggling, and suddenly she felt a bit like Alice and wondered when she'd slipped down the rabbit hole.

Hank made small talk on the short walk to the cottage, commenting on the property along with the heat and humidity.

Grace led Hank into Charlotte's sitting area and gestured to the sofa. Built in 1835, the cottage had once been used as a chapel. When Grace and Charlotte purchased the property, they converted it into Charlotte's living quarters. It was a small house, and the combination living room and bedroom worked for Charlotte. But sometimes her sister wished for a bigger kitchen when late-night inspiration struck.

Grace had always felt at peace in the cottage, and now she drew on its quiet strength. "Can I get you something to drink?" She couldn't believe she was playing hostess to her long-dead husband.

"Relax. You don't have to wait on me like a guest." Hank sat down on the sofa and regarded the room. "This is nice. I like the beams. It's very old-world." He frowned. "It's a little small for the owner of the inn, but I guess it's suitable for you."

"Actually, this is Charlotte's place," Grace answered. "I have quarters in the mansion."

He nodded but didn't say anything.

Grace dropped into a chair before her legs could give out on her. It was all too much to comprehend. "This is crazy. It's like something out of a movie." She hoped that any minute she'd wake up from this bizarre dream.

"It's crazy but real," Hank said as he reached for her.

Grace scooted back in her chair to avoid his touch. She couldn't help it. Technically he was her husband—or maybe he wasn't, but that was a legal nightmare for another day—but he was also a stranger.

He flinched at her rejection.

"I have a million questions," Grace said. "How can you be alive? Where have you been? Why didn't you come home twenty-two years ago? Were you a spy, and I didn't know it?" If he said yes, that would be the easiest truth to accept, but she knew it wasn't the answer.

"Let's go with one question at a time," Hank said.

"Where have you been all this time?" Grace asked. It came out harsher than she intended. But who could blame her? She hadn't heard a single word from him in more than twenty years. Then suddenly he showed up on her doorstep. How was she supposed to react?

"Vienna, Austria."

Grace rolled his answer over in her mind and was privately amused by life's twisted sense of humor. A few years after Hank's alleged passing, she'd been working on an account headquartered in Vienna for her job at Maddox Creative in Charleston. She'd declined several invitations to visit the flagship hotel. If she had traveled there, maybe she would have seen him. Shaking her head, she shoved the useless thought aside and focused on the questions crowding her brain.

"How did you survive the train crash?" Her stomach burned and twisted as the horrible memories resurfaced. So many people had been lost that day. If it hadn't been for her family's love and support... Well, some things were better left in the past.

"I think my guardian angel was working overtime," Hank said, then grew somber. "Honestly, I don't know. My business partners weren't so lucky. When the rescue workers found me, I was knocked out. They transported me to the hospital, and it was touch and go for about ten days."

"What happened next?"

He pressed his thumb and forefinger to his eyes and took a deep breath. "When I finally woke up, I had no memory of my life. I couldn't picture you or Jake. I didn't even know my own name. There was nothing. Just a black void."

The story tore at Grace's heart. Tears burned her eyes. She'd lost her husband. He'd lost everything. "But how did you get to Austria?" She had to fight the emotion tearing her up inside to get the question out.

"The details are still a little fuzzy from those early days," Hank answered. "But when they found me, I was clinging to a messenger bag that they thought was mine. The train ticket inside was issued to Gustav Heinz from Vienna. When they started to ask me questions in German, I could answer, so they assumed it was me."

"Muscle memory?" Grace asked. "You always did have a knack for languages, and you excelled in German in high school and college."

"It's why I was sent on that dreadful trip in the first place."

They sat for a moment, letting his words sink in.

Once again, she indulged in what-ifs. What if Hank hadn't gone on that trip? What if Hank hadn't been the only engineer at his firm who spoke fluent German? What if she'd asked him not to go?

Grace pushed the thoughts away and asked, "What happened after you got out of the hospital?"

He chuckled. "I hesitantly got on another train and headed to Vienna. Except I had no idea where I lived or what I did. So I found a job as a waiter and moved into a tiny room at a shabby hotel. The ceiling leaked, and the walls were thinner than paper. Eventually I made a friend, and we got a flat together. It wasn't much better, but at least it didn't rain inside."

"Your memory didn't return?" she asked.

"Not really."

"During all those years, nothing jogged your memory of us? Of home?" Grace wondered if it was really so easy to forget the people you loved.

"There were times when I'd see someone and get this funny feeling like I should remember someone or something, but it was always out of my grasp." Hank reached out again, stopped a few inches from touching her, and dropped his hand.

"That's awful. I don't know how you dealt with it for so long." She'd always heard that traumatic amnesia, the kind caused by a blow to the head, was only temporary. Apparently she'd been wrong.

"I searched frantically for the first couple of years," he admitted. "But I realized it would drive me crazy. So I had to accept the fact that something was missing from my life and move on."

"You did the right thing," Grace assured him. "It was probably the only thing you could have done. No one would blame you for giving up and creating a life for yourself."

"I had to bury my desire to rediscover my old life for a while," Hank said. "But I never really gave up."

"That's true. You're here now." Grace tilted her head. "How did that happen? I would think that your memories would be gone for good after such a long time."

"I guess that guardian angel thought I was ready." He suddenly jumped off the sofa and paced around the room like a caged cat. Nervous energy came off him in waves.

This had to be as hard for Hank as it was for her. She remained silent and let him take his time.

Hank picked up a knickknack and set it back down, then grabbed one of Charlotte's cookbooks and thumbed through the pages. "This is what brought it all back." He laughed, holding up the book.

"Charlotte's cookbook?" Grace asked. Her sister had written several best-selling cookbooks, and she was currently working on a new one. "I don't understand the connection."

"I heard a tourist in the restaurant where I worked talking about her meal," Hank explained. "She compared it to a dish she'd made from a cookbook written by Charlotte Wylde. She mentioned the author owned an inn in South Carolina with her sister, Grace Porter."

Grace gasped. "Hearing my name was all it took for you to remember?"

"I wish it had been that easy," he answered. "Your name had to go through layers to get to my subconscious. That night my dreams were flooded with images of the most beautiful woman I'd ever seen. And there was a little boy. We were at the beach building a sandcastle. We had an amazing life together."

She sifted through her memories. "We went to the beach the weekend before you left. We built the sandcastle, and then you and Jake played Godzilla and destroyed it, laughing the whole time."

"I remember." Hank knelt down in front of her and took her hands. "I woke up in the morning with tears in my eyes. I remembered everything. You. Jake. Our life. I had all my memories back."

Grace slowly pulled her hands free as she processed Hank's story. It was definitely not a hoax. He was really here.

"As soon as I could, I reserved the Wisteria Loft Suite under the name Gustav Heinz," he said. "I came here straight from the airport because I couldn't wait to see you."

"I need some air." Without waiting for a response, Grace ran from the cottage, her heart pounding. She stood outside the door and breathed deeply. When she was sure that she wouldn't pass out, she turned to go back inside.

Hank watched her from the doorway. "It's a lot to take in."

She nodded, not trusting her voice.

"I'll give you some time. I'm not going anywhere, so you can come to me when you're ready." He followed the path to the inn.

Grace felt rooted to the spot. If only Spencer were home. He'd make sense out of all this.

No, she couldn't go there. How was she going to tell Spencer that her husband was alive? After getting to know each other, they'd finally gone on a few dates. They'd been taking it slowly. Despite what she always said to her sister, Spencer was definitely more than just a friend.

She collapsed onto the bench outside Charlotte's cottage. What was she going to do? Grace had loved Hank, but that was a lifetime ago. Even though the man who'd stood before her today was her husband, she didn't know him anymore. Twenty-two years was a long time to be apart. She wasn't the same person she was back then, and he wasn't either. They'd lived entire lives since they'd last seen each other.

She'd mourned the man she'd lost, but she'd eventually moved on.

But Hank was her husband, and they'd exchanged vows. Grace needed to honor those promises.

Yet she felt a sinking sensation. There was something about Hank's tale, his reaction, his tears, the timbre of his voice that didn't quite ring true.

She shivered, wondering if she should trust him. Exactly how much had he changed?

Grace

When Grace walked into the kitchen the next morning with Winston, she found Charlotte busy preparing breakfast. Bacon was sizzling on the stove, and a savory aroma came from the oven.

Charlotte glanced up from kneading dough. "Coffee's ready if you want some."

"Thanks." Grace retrieved a mug from the cabinet and poured herself a cup of the rich brew.

Winston whined.

"Don't worry. I haven't forgotten about you." Grace set her cup down and poured kibble into the dog's bowl, then refreshed his water.

Winston eagerly dug in.

The back door opened, and Winnie entered the kitchen.

A comforting warmth spread through Grace at her aunt's arrival. "It's great to see you."

"You too." Winnie hugged Grace and Charlotte.

Already finished with his breakfast, Winston bounded over to Winnie and wagged his tail.

Winnie smiled as she scratched behind the dog's ears. "How are you girls this morning?"

"Busy," Grace replied. "There's a lot to do with a full inn."

"What are you making?" Winnie asked her other niece.

Charlotte swiped a loose strand of hair off her cheek with her forearm as she worked the dough. "Cinnamon scones, homemade whipped cream, and fresh berries. And there's a quiche in the oven."

"Sounds wonderful," Winnie remarked as she poured herself a cup of coffee.

A level of exhaustion hummed throughout the room. Grace studied her aunt, noticing the dark smudges under her eyes. Charlotte appeared to have everything under control, but her usual perky smile was missing, and her quick and efficient movements were a bit more measured. It wasn't surprising. Yesterday's shock affected them all.

"I'll set out the breakfast dishes," Winnie offered.

Grace gathered the table linens and headed to the veranda. It was going to be a beautiful day, so their guests could dine alfresco this morning.

She and her aunt set the tables for breakfast in companionable silence. As they worked, Grace replayed Hank's story for the thousandth time. She'd spent the night running it through her mind over and over as she tossed and turned and punched her pillow. She'd finally gotten up and studied her wedding picture.

For so long Grace had prayed for a miracle—that the officials had been wrong and Hank was alive. She'd held out hope even as she'd planned his memorial service with a broken heart. Somewhere along the way, she'd accepted his death and learned to live without the man she loved. She raised their son, enjoyed a successful career, and started a new one. A new life.

Whoever was working in the miracle-granting department was a bit behind the curve, because twenty-two years was a long wait. Too long. Once again, her life was in upheaval, and Grace did not like chaos.

Not that she was sorry Hank was alive.

She sent another silent thank-you that Jake had his father back. The thought alone brought tears to her eyes. She had to take a deep breath as she snapped another cloth napkin and refolded it.

I need to call Jake, but how do I tell him that his father's alive?

"I'm going to see if Charlotte needs any help," Winnie said, then went inside.

Monty and Jamie stepped out onto the veranda.

Grace pushed her problems aside. She'd deal with those issues later, but right now she had guests to attend to. "Good morning. Would anyone like some coffee? Charlotte will have breakfast ready shortly, and we'll be serving it buffet style."

"Coffee sounds good," Lucinda said as she joined them. "Goodness, I don't remember the last time I slept so late. If I were at home I would have been up hours ago. I feel like a lady of luxury."

The others laughed, and the Robinsons agreed they'd slept wonderfully, which was music to Grace's ears. She was pleased to know that her guests were content and well rested.

"This is how every morning should start," Jamie said. "It's so pretty here."

Beaming with pride, Grace said, "Thank you. I'm glad you think so. And I hope everyone is hungry this morning." She rattled off the day's breakfast menu. "Of course, if you have any specific dietary needs or there's something else you'd prefer, Charlotte will be happy to make it for you."

Charlotte brought out a tray of scones, cream, and berries. "There she goes again, volunteering me for all the work," she joked. "So typical of big sisters."

"Everything sounds great," Jamie said. "I hate to ask, but could I have tea instead of coffee? Earl Grey if you have it."

"Of course." Charlotte flashed the group a smile. "I'll let Grace get that for you. Would anyone like something other than quiche? Scrambled eggs? Cereal or yogurt? I thought tomorrow I'd make French toast or maybe Belgium waffles, unless anyone objects."

Jamie groaned. "I'll have to go on a diet when I get home, but it'll be worth every bite."

"You're perfect exactly the way you are," Monty said, gazing adoringly at his wife. "You're as beautiful today—even more so—as you were the day we met twenty-eight years ago."

"Flattery will not get you a second scone," Jamie said as she playfully elbowed him.

Monty sighed and kissed her cheek. "You can't blame a man for trying."

The sisters left the guests for a moment to run back to the kitchen for the rest of the food. Grace put the kettle on for tea.

"Monty looks at his wife the way Spencer looks at you." Charlotte sliced the quiche resting on the counter. "Speaking of Spencer, is he back home?"

"Not yet." Grace didn't want to think about Spencer because then she'd also have to think about Hank and the jumbled mess of emotions running rampant through her heart and head.

She stared out the window as she waited for the water to boil. Monty's expression hadn't gone unnoticed by her either. It was *the* look, the one that said Jamie was his world, his heart, his soul, the one he'd sacrifice everything for. Grace believed every woman should experience that look at least once in her lifetime.

Did Spencer look at her that way? No, it was too early in their relationship for those deep feelings, but she had been its recipient a long time ago. If Hank had loved her like that—truly, madly, deeply—how was it possible that he had forgotten about her and their child for more than twenty years?

None of this made sense.

"Are you all right?" Charlotte touched her sleeve, concern etched around her eyes. "The water is boiling. Why don't I handle breakfast, and you take some time for yourself this morning?"

Grace smiled, moved by her sister's offer and so thankful that she had Charlotte and Winnie by her side. "I'm okay, but thank you. Where's Winnie?"

"I don't know. When she was in the kitchen with me earlier, she said she had to take care of something, but she'd be back." Charlotte motioned toward the center island. "Can you grab the juice for me? I'll bring out the second wave when the Bensons and Hank come down."

"We have another guest checking in today," Grace reminded her as she picked up the juice. "Christie Thompson."

Charlotte balanced the loaded tray and opened the kitchen door. "Right, she's in the Rosebud Suite. It's all ready for her arrival. I popped in there earlier and double-checked everything."

"You've certainly been busy this morning," Grace remarked as she followed her sister to the veranda.

"There's something about a full house that invigorates me."

Grace suspected it had more to do with not being able to sleep, but she kept the comment to herself.

When they walked onto the veranda, the Robinsons and Lucinda were chatting, but they all stopped to compliment Charlotte on the beautiful quiche and the delicious scones.

"Lucinda was telling us about her rooster," Monty said as he helped himself to a large slice of quiche.

Jamie shook her head and grinned at her husband. "Apparently, the conversation is making you hungry."

He chuckled.

"I've been trying to talk Grace into getting chickens," Charlotte said. "We'd have a steady supply of eggs, and they're really good at pest control."

"But they'll get you up at the crack of dawn," Lucinda said.

Charlotte laughed, waving the comment off. "I'm already up then."

"Well, I'm not," Grace said. "And I'm fond of sleeping."

"Me too," Lucinda said. "If you get a rooster, I won't be able to come back here and sleep in."

The group laughed.

Joel walked onto the veranda and greeted them. "I'd like to make up a couple of plates and take them to my room. I thought it would be nice for Felicity to enjoy breakfast in bed."

The Robinsons exchanged knowing glances and focused on their breakfast.

Lucinda's blue eyes lit up. "Young man, if you keep doing that, you'll enjoy many wonderful years with your bride."

"Thank you," Joel said with a smile. "That's what I'm aiming for."

"My Charley, bless his soul, used to surprise me all the time," Lucinda said.

"How so?" Joel asked as he poured juice into two glasses.

"For birthdays and anniversaries, he'd take me out to fancy dinners and the movies or shows I wanted to see," Lucinda replied. "Those were all fine and dandy, but it was the small gestures that kept stealing my heart."

"Like breakfast in bed?" Joel asked.

Lucinda smiled. "That and more. Picking fresh flowers and leaving them around the house. Having coffee ready for me in the morning because he set up the coffee maker the night before. Always stopping at a bookstore because he knew I was happiest with a book in my hand. Doing the dishes for me or even something as simple as asking me to come outside so we could watch the sunset together."

Jamie pressed her hand to her chest. "He sounds like a man very much in love."

"I was very much in love too," Lucinda said. "It's been three years since he passed, and I still miss him every day."

Grace had to blink away tears before she made a scene. Glancing around, she noticed that she wasn't the only one affected by Lucinda's words.

Charlotte excused herself to get warm scones and quiche for Joel. Grace helped him load his tray with silverware and condiments. She plucked a rosebud out of one of the vases and set it on the tray for him.

The lone flower brought back wonderful memories. When Grace and Hank were newly married, money was tight, and they couldn't afford bouquets from a florist. But Hank had found a way to give her fresh flowers by making an agreement with one of their neighbors. Hank carried the neighbor's trash cans to the curb, and in exchange she let him cut flowers from her garden. Twice a week, a single bud appeared at the breakfast table or on Grace's nightstand. Once she'd found a flower in her briefcase. She hoped Felicity appreciated the sweet gesture.

Before Grace could go too far down memory lane, Monty and Jamie asked her advice on local sites to visit. As Grace told them about the various shops, museums, and historical must-sees, her gaze strayed to Lucinda. A few minutes ago, the older woman had been laughing and engaged, but now she turned away from the others and pushed her half-eaten breakfast to the side.

Grace made a mental note to seek her out after breakfast to make sure everything was okay. Being a widow didn't come with an instruction manual, and she knew too well how hard those first several years could be, even though she supposed she wasn't technically a widow anymore. Actually, she never had been. *Something else to get used to.*

Charlotte returned with two covered plates for Joel.

A minute later, Winnie breezed onto the veranda, appearing unusually disheveled. Several strands of hair hung loose from her bun, and dust streaked her shirt and her right cheek.

"What have you been up to?" Grace asked her aunt.

Winnie shrugged. "Oh, you know me. A little of this and a little of that."

Grace glanced at Charlotte and read matching confusion in her expression.

Winnie walked over to Lucinda. "I'm so glad you're still out here."

"Did you need me for something, Mrs. Bennett?"

"Please call me Winnie. Actually, I have something for you. I was afraid I'd miss you because it took me so long. Anyway, this is for you." She handed Lucinda an old-fashioned gold compass.

Lucinda took the item and turned it over in her hands. She opened and closed it before shaking her head. "I don't understand. This isn't mine."

"It is now," Winnie said with a smile, then turned to Grace. "I'm going to start on the rooms."

"I'll be up in a moment. I need to take care of something first." Grace intended to slip into her private quarters and contact Jake. She'd tried calling him last night, and she'd been almost relieved when he hadn't answered. But Grace couldn't put it off any longer. She needed to break the news to her son, even though she wished she could do it in person. Jake lived in Raleigh, so she didn't have a choice.

Hank walked onto the veranda and flashed the group a wide smile. "Good morning, everyone. My apologies for oversleeping. Jet lag."

Grace wondered why he felt the need to explain his sleeping in, then reproached herself for reading into his words.

"How can I help?" Hank asked Grace. "Do you want me to cook? Do dishes? Please put me to work. After all, I need to start learning how to run an inn."

Winnie and Charlotte froze, their gaze zeroed in on him. Grace was every bit as stunned as they were. Joel quickly excused himself and returned to his room with his breakfast tray. Monty and Jamie shifted in their seats to focus on their breakfast and talk quietly. Lucinda pressed her lips together as she stared at Hank.

Grace thought the older woman's reaction was interesting. She must have overheard Hank's arrival the day before.

Charlotte cleared her throat but didn't say anything.

Grace realized she hadn't responded to Hank, but she honestly didn't know what to tell him. The idea of Hank running the inn with her and Charlotte hadn't even crossed her mind. She was still trying to get used to the idea that he was alive. There hadn't been time to consider what it meant as far as his playing an active role in her life and business. She needed time and space to come to terms with this bizarre situation.

"Thank you for the offer, but we've got it under control," Grace told Hank. "Please enjoy your breakfast, everyone."

If her feet had moved any faster exiting the veranda, they would have sprouted wings.

Winston followed, obviously concerned about his mistress.

Grace entered her private quarters. She shut the door behind her dog and leaned against it. "What am I going to do?" she whispered to Winston.

If he had an answer, he kept it to himself.

Christie

As Christie Thompson turned into the driveway of the Magnolia Harbor Inn, her phone pinged with an incoming text for what had to be the tenth time since she'd left home that morning. After checking the first couple of messages and seeing that they weren't emergencies, she ignored the phone and the pleas of Blake Dalton, her ex-boyfriend.

She parked her car under the shade of a giant oak tree and regarded the beautiful inn. The antebellum mansion would have looked at home in the pages of a history book. The three-story building featured a large wraparound porch on the lower and upper levels, tall white columns, and numerous windows. According to her research, it had been built in 1816.

As a history lover and genealogist, Christie wished the walls could talk. She had started asking questions and spinning stories the minute she'd booked her stay. Who had built the house? Was it filled with love and laughter?

In her version of the story, the third and youngest son of a British duke was tired of living in his brothers' shadows and following his father's strict edicts, so he struck out for America with his new bride. As a favorite of his grandparents, the duke had a generous trust, which allowed him to purchase the land surrounding Lake Haven, where he built a grand house for his love. They filled their home with children, and the manor was passed down through the generations until the children moved away or hard times fell upon the family. Christie hadn't quite decided how their story ended.

Maybe she'd figure it out before her trip was over.

For now, she grabbed her purse and phone and got out of the car. She took a moment to stretch, then called her sister. She'd promised to let Carly know as soon as she arrived. Her own mother wasn't nearly as much of a mother hen as her sister. The phone rang twice before Carly answered.

"I thought you'd never call," Carly said, worry evident in her voice.

Christie rolled her eyes but smiled, even though Carly could see neither action. "I just got here, and I'm right on time. Exactly three hours and thirty minutes from when I left my house."

Her sister let out a deep sigh. "I know, but it's a long drive by yourself, and a lot can happen."

"That's why I have roadside assistance," Christie replied. "Honestly, it was an easy drive and so beautiful. I couldn't have asked for a nicer day." She frowned. "Well, except for the part where my phone was blowing up."

"What do you mean?" Carly asked. "Is something wrong?"

She leaned back against her car. "No, it's Blake. He's begging me to give him a second chance."

"Maybe you should."

"He had three whole years to decide if I was the one," Christie reminded her. "But he hasn't proposed, which tells me I'm not his one and only. It's time for me to move on."

Frustrated, she spun around and kicked the tire of her car. This wasn't how she'd seen her life going—alone and starting over. All signs had pointed to Blake being the guy for her, but she couldn't have been more wrong.

"Maybe he's just not ready for marriage," Carly suggested.

"I don't think he'll ever be ready," Christie said. "His buddies are more important to him than our relationship ever was. He made that very clear. I need someone who is going to put me first. A guy who isn't going to freak out over the idea of someday having kids and whose idea of a savings account is in a bank, not a mason jar."

"I understand," Carly said. "But Blake's a great guy, and he cares about you."

Christie remained silent and let her sister ramble on about Blake's virtues, not that she needed Carly or anyone else to tell her. Everyone liked Blake. Her ex was a genuinely nice guy. He held doors open for complete strangers and helped people who needed it—be it with cranky kids, runaway dogs, or heavy bags. Blake had a smile for every person he saw, and every stranger was a friend he hadn't met yet.

Christie didn't dislike the guy. She liked him a lot. In fact, she loved him. If he'd asked her a month ago to marry him, she would have said yes in a heartbeat. But he hadn't. Instead, when she'd asked him about marriage, he'd brushed the topic aside and told her that he was in no big hurry. Christie was thirty-two, and all she could think about was her biological clock ticking. If she intended to have children someday—and she did—she couldn't sit around and wait for a thirty-four-year-old boy to grow up.

Not if she wanted to beat the family curse. Both her mom and grandmother had gone through menopause early, and her doctor said chances were high that Christie would as well. Christie feared that time was running out for her to have children of her own.

"I know you're a hopeless romantic," Christie said. "But promise me you're not going to tell Blake where I'm staying. If I'm to have any hope of moving on and finding someone else, I need Blake to stop dropping by all the time. He needs to believe that I'm over him and getting on with my life."

"If it's so hard for you to move on," Carly said, "it might be a sign that you're not supposed to."

"Come on. Promise me."

"Fine." Carly sighed. "I promise."

Christie popped the trunk, then grabbed her suitcase and computer bag. "I wish you were here. It's gorgeous. There are oak and magnolia trees and Spanish moss and flowers everywhere. It's like a postcard, and I haven't even seen inside the inn or the lake yet."

"It sounds like my kind of place. I'd love to be there with my sketch pad," Carly said. "It's a shame we're so busy at work."

"Well, if that changes, don't forget that it's not very far away. It would be great to have you here."

"Even with my nagging about Blake?" Carly teased.

Christie laughed as she hiked her computer bag onto her shoulder. "Even with your nagging."

"I want you to be happy," Carly said more seriously. "And I know you were happy with him."

"True, but I want more, and we plateaued," Christie said. "Anyway, think about my offer, even for a night or two. We haven't done a sister getaway in ages."

"Take lots of pictures just in case I can't make it."

"I will," Christie said. "But right now, I'm going to get checked in. Then I'm heading to the library to start my genealogy project."

"Good luck and call me later. I want to hear how it goes."

Christie promised to do so and hung up. She slipped her phone into her pocket and walked to the front door. As she opened it, a little bell jingled overhead.

The cutest dog on the planet came running to greet her. He plopped down at her feet and gazed at her adoringly.

Christie smiled. "What's your name?" She held out her hand for the dog to sniff. Once he did and gave her hand a lick, she bent down to pet him. He leaned into her, tail wagging as if she were an old friend he hadn't seen in ages.

"That's Winston. Our official greeter, king of the castle, and snuggle bug," a blonde woman said as she entered the room. "Welcome to the Magnolia Harbor Inn. I'm Charlotte Wylde, one of the owners."

Christie set her bags on the floor and picked up Winston. "I'm Christie Thompson. I have a reservation."

Charlotte nodded. "You're in our Rosebud Suite, which has a queen-size bed and a view of the garden. It shares a bathroom with the Bluebell Suite, but I think you'll like the guest staying in there. Lucinda Grayson is lovely."

"That sounds nice, and I'm sure I'll get along fine with her." Christie gave Winston some more love, then straightened. "Actually, I probably won't be around much during the day."

"Are you here visiting family or friends?" Charlotte asked, walking over to the reception desk.

"I'm on a working vacation," Christie said. "I'm doing some genealogy research for a client. Hopefully I'll be able to dig up some information on her ancestors."

"That must be fun and challenging," Charlotte remarked.

"You have no idea."

Charlotte gave her a questioning glance.

"Their last name is Riley," Christie said. "It's like searching for a needle in a haystack."

Charlotte handed her a registration form to fill out. "It sounds like you won't have any free time to actually enjoy the vacation part of your trip."

That was exactly what Christie was hoping for. She wanted to remain busy so she wouldn't have time to think about Blake. Walking away from him had almost broken her. She loved the guy, but she wasn't going to stay his girlfriend forever. Life was too short, and she wanted so much more.

She wrote down the information and returned the form to Charlotte. "It's okay. I could use the distraction right now."

"If you need any help, be sure to ask Phyllis Gendel at the Heritage Library. She's the head librarian, and she knows everything about everyone who has ever lived here." Charlotte laughed and shook her head. "It's one of the joys of living in a small town."

"Thanks for the tip. I'm sure I'll be utilizing her services." Before Christie could say anything else, her phone pinged with a missed call. She pulled the phone out of her pocket and groaned when she saw Blake's number.

"Is everything okay?" Charlotte asked as she retrieved Christie's suitcase.

"Yes. No." Laughing, Christie picked up her computer bag. "I wish I could find a nice guy who isn't afraid of making a real commitment. You wouldn't happen to know any, would you?"

"I completely understand," Charlotte said as she headed to the stairs. "I used to feel the same way, like all the nice guys had already been taken."

"Sounds like you've had a change of heart." Christie followed her hostess up the curved staircase to the second floor and down the hallway.

Winston scampered after them.

"I have." Charlotte stopped in front of the door to the Rosebud Suite and opened it. "Here it is."

When Christie entered the room, she instantly fell in love with it. The suite featured gleaming hardwood floors, plenty of windows, a four-poster bed fit for a queen, and an armchair next to a gas fireplace. She could easily spend hours doing genealogy research in her room and never feel cooped up. "This is gorgeous," she gushed.

"Thanks. That's what we like to hear." Charlotte rolled the suitcase to a corner and smoothed a nonexistent wrinkle on the bed. "As for changing my mind, I finally found someone, and it was the last person I expected."

"Really? Care to share your secrets?" Christie sat on the armchair and gave it a little bounce. Comfy. Yep, this was a great spot to work and relax.

Winston hopped up on her lap.

"Believe it or not, he was right in front of me the whole time," Charlotte said. "Of course, I couldn't see it at first. I even signed up for a matchmaking service. Guess who they paired me with?"

"The guy you're dating now?" Christie asked as she scratched behind the dog's ears.

"The very one. I thought it was a practical joke. We didn't exactly get along back then. Dean Bradley's the chef and owner of The Tidewater across the lake, and we can be a little competitive. We had worked together before and developed quite the rivalry. He's good, but I'm better." Charlotte grinned. "That's between us girls."

They shared a conspiratorial smile.

"If you go to The Tidewater, let them know you're a guest here," Charlotte said. "Dean will go out of his way to impress you."

"So I'll get the VIP treatment?" Christie asked with a smile.

"Probably. He'll want you to come back bragging about his food."

They both laughed.

Maybe this wouldn't be such a lonely vacation after all. Christie might not experience the romantic getaway she'd hoped for or even the fun sister retreat, but she had a feeling she was going to make a new friend at the Magnolia Harbor Inn.

"If you're serious about finding someone who's ready to commit, maybe you should consider a matchmaking service," Charlotte suggested.

"I've thought about it," Christie admitted. She'd looked into a few online dating sites, but something kept holding her back. "It feels overwhelming."

"Kind of like dating." Charlotte gave the room one last glance. "I could give you the name of the service I used. They're based in Charleston, but they serve all over the South. They do a great job of screening their applicants."

"Let me think about it, and I'll let you know."

"Of course," Charlotte said. "Take your time. We're here to help. If that's not for you, that's okay too. My sister says I can be bossy sometimes, and I'm sorry if that's how I came across."

"No need to apologize. I appreciate your offer," Christie said. "But I'm torn. I want to move on. My head says to move on, but my heart doesn't agree."

Grace

Grace collapsed on her bed and exhaled. Most days she thrived on the demands of owning an inn, but today she had been anxiously waiting for this quiet moment.

Restless, she got up and paced around her small living room. With breakfast over, the morning chores done, and the last guest checked in, she finally had a few minutes to herself. Grace could no longer delay her call to Jake.

Once again, she wished she could break the news to her son in person. If they didn't have a full inn, she would drive to Raleigh, but she couldn't burden Charlotte with all the tasks. Running the place was a full-time job for both of them. Plus, she didn't feel right leaving with Hank here.

Technically, she supposed Hank was her husband, but he'd been gone for a lifetime. Legally, she wasn't sure if he was her husband. He'd been declared dead. Not that it mattered. The inn belonged to her and Charlotte. His earlier comment about learning to run the business scraped at the edges of her nerves. It was presumptuous. They hadn't talked about their relationship or future, and for Hank to make such a comment in front of Charlotte and her aunt, not to mention their guests, was inappropriate.

Calculated.

Now why did that word pop into her head? Something kept niggling at the back of Grace's mind just out of reach, and it wouldn't let her find any peace. Reviewing Hank's words and actions didn't point to anything specifically suspicious, but warning bells were going off left and right. Granted, Grace realized she was still in shock over his reappearance.

"My head and heart are overreacting, trying to protect me from getting hurt again," she told Winston who had been watching her pace across the room.

Winston barked three times before he settled down on his doggy bed.

"A nap does sound like a good idea, but first I need to talk to Jake." She retrieved her tablet and sent her son a text.

He responded immediately and said he was working from home. If she couldn't talk to him in person, a video call was the next best thing.

Grace settled into her overstuffed chair with a throw pillow in her lap and her favorite hot tea next to her. Taking a deep breath, she said a prayer for strength and called Jake.

A few seconds later, her handsome son's smile lit up the screen. "I'm sorry I missed you last night. I would have called you back, but I got in really late and figured you had already turned in."

"Were you out with the guys?" she asked.

"No, I was on a date."

"Really? Want to tell me about her?"

Jake's smile cranked up a notch. "It was a first date. She's really nice, and we'll see what happens from here. If we go out again, then I'll tell you all about her."

Grace's heart warmed at her son's obvious happiness. "Fair enough."

"How's everything there? You look a little tired."

How could Grace answer his question? That the last twenty-four hours had been emotional? Stressful? Shocking? All of the above? She reminded herself to be thankful. Jake had lost too many years with his father, and now he had the chance to try to make up for them.

"Everything's fine. We've got a full inn this week, which is a good thing, but that means more work." She paused. "Would you be able to come home for a few days?"

"I can't. I'm up against a major project deadline." Jake edged closer to the computer screen, eyes narrowed in suspicion. "You said everything's fine. You only say that when you don't want me to worry. What's going on?"

"I have some news for you. It's good news, but it will come as a shock. I'd rather tell you in person, but since neither of us can make the drive right now—"

"Are you and Spencer getting married?" Jake interrupted, frowning.

Her son's expression concerned her, but at the moment she didn't have the time or energy to think about the meaning behind it. "Of course not. We've only been on a few dates." She pressed her fingers to her forehead. Her relationship with Spencer was another thing she needed to figure out. If only he weren't in D.C. She'd give anything to hear his voice. It took every ounce of willpower not to call him. "This is about your dad."

Jake grinned. "After all these years, did you find out there's a secret trust left to me?"

"Well, as it turns out . . . I don't know how to say this, except there was a mistake."

"What kind of mistake?" Jake asked. "Is the insurance company trying to take back the money or something?"

"What?" she asked, stunned by yet another new complication. Surely the insurance company would demand repayment. That shouldn't be a problem, because it hadn't been a huge payout and she'd built up a nice nest egg for her retirement. But what if they pressed charges or sent her a bill for interest? She needed to make an appointment with her lawyer. "No, that's not it."

"Then what is it?" he asked.

There was no easy way to say it, so she'd better just spit out the truth. "He's not dead."

Jake remained silent as a myriad of emotions crossed his face. "I don't understand. If he's alive, where has he been all this time? How do you know he's alive?" He quickly picked up his mug, and coffee sloshed over the side.

"Are you all right?"

"Yeah, just surprised."

Grace took a sip of her tea. "We all are." She filled her son in on how Hank had arrived at the inn, then related his story of where he'd been for the past twenty-two years and what had happened that fateful day.

When she was done, they both sat there in silence for a moment.

"I'm so sorry to break the news like this," Grace said. "But I had to tell you as soon as possible. You've already missed so many years with your dad, and I didn't want you to lose any more time."

"Thanks for telling me," he said. "It's kind of a fantastic story."

"What do you mean?"

Jake shrugged. "It seems a little far-fetched, but what do I know? I'm just glad he's alive and back home."

She nodded.

"We're at a crucial point on this project," he said. "But I'll talk to my boss this morning and see if I can get away for a few days. It might not be until next week. We're all hands on deck right now."

"That's fine."

Grace's door opened, and Hank strolled into the room.

"Hey, Jake," Hank said, leaning into Grace's space. "How's my boy?"

Grace scooted over to give him some room. "Honey, this is your dad."

"Hi. Uh, it's nice to meet you." Jake glanced from her to Hank.

"So your mom told you what happened, right?" Hank asked.

"She did. It's quite the story," Jake said. "Look, I don't mean to be rude, but I need to get back to work. We've got a big deadline. I'll see you soon. Bye, Mom. Love you." He disconnected.

Grace set the tablet down and bowed her head in prayer. She needed guidance and strength, and her heart told her so did Jake. Dropping a bombshell on her son over video chat was bad enough. But the way Hank had popped into the room as if it were no big deal, as if he had always been there, was unacceptable. Didn't he realize what a shock his reappearance was to everyone? Especially to Jake, who had only been a little boy when he lost his father?

Grace stood and faced Hank. "What do you think you're doing?" She crossed the room and closed the door to make sure their conversation was kept private, something he didn't seem to grasp.

"Saying hello to my son," Hank replied.

They needed to discuss the situation, their relationship, and boundaries. But Grace wasn't ready. She still needed time to deal with all these changes and decipher how she felt about the man standing before her. Even though it wasn't the right time to discuss everything, she decided to clear up a few things.

Grace took a deep breath and plunged ahead. "I understand that you're excited to be home and have your family back."

"Is there something wrong with that?"

"No, of course not. But you need to remember that we're still processing your return," she said. "Jake found out that his father was alive merely seconds before you walked into my private quarters and talked to him. You were dead for most of his life. He's used to not having a father. It's a lot for him to take in, and I think it would have gone better if you had waited."

"I've waited a long time," Hank said. "Besides, he's not a child anymore."

"Well, technically, you didn't wait that long because you only remembered us last week," she pointed out.

Instead of responding to her comment, he glanced around her living quarters and said, "So this is your room. It's even smaller than Charlotte's cottage."

Grace had an entire inn at her disposal, so she didn't need much space. When she wanted privacy, her small living room nook suited her fine. "Yes, this is *my* room. I'd appreciate it if next time you'd knock before entering."

Hank met her eyes. "My apologies. I assumed there was no need to knock since you're my wife."

"We haven't actually been husband and wife for some time," she said. "I know we need to talk about us, but it's a little too soon. Can we table that discussion for another time?"

"Sure. I'm in no hurry."

"Also, if you could please refrain from making personal comments in front of the other guests, Charlotte and I would appreciate it."

"Of course. Maybe I'll take one of the kayaks out on the lake. Get out of your way and let you do your thing while I try to figure out how to get my life back." Hank stormed out of the room.

She sighed. Her emotions felt scattered all over the place. She picked up Winston and cuddled her dog. "I'm glad he's alive, but I really could do without all the drama."

Grace allowed herself a good long snuggle with Winston while she finished her lukewarm tea. She refused to dwell on the conversation with Hank. She needed to pull herself together and get some things done around the inn, like fixing the dryer.

After exiting her room, Grace went into the kitchen and spied a note from her sister on the island. Charlotte had gone into town to run a few errands, but she'd be back in time to prepare the evening's appetizers.

Walking to the front door, she scanned the front parking area to see that Christie's and the Bensons' cars were gone, which meant she had at least three guests in the house. Maybe she should set a pitcher of lemonade and a plate of cookies on the back veranda before tackling the dryer.

Monty and Jamie descended the stairs. They were holding hands and laughing, and they seemed more like a young couple on their honeymoon than parents about to see their son graduate from college.

"We're glad we caught you," Jamie said. "We probably won't be able to attend the hospitality hour tonight."

"Are there some events at the college today?" Grace jotted down a note to Charlotte at the front desk, letting her know not to expect the Robinsons. Not that it would stop her sister from making too much food.

"Not today," Monty said. "I'm taking Jamie out to explore the area, and then we have reservations for dinner at Turner's Lakeside Grill."

Grace smiled. "Sounds like you have a lovely day ahead. Turner's has a wonderful rib eye that will melt in your mouth, and their grilled swordfish is perfection."

"Thanks for the recommendations," Monty said. "We'll keep them in mind."

The couple waved as they left.

Returning to the kitchen, Grace prepared a pitcher of lemonade and arranged molasses cookies on a plate. She delivered them to the back veranda, then headed to the laundry room to tackle the menace known as the dryer.

She couldn't help certain thoughts from occupying her mind. Never before had she had a houseful of guests that so completely represented her life: what it had been, what it could have been, and what it might be.

The Bensons, so young and in love, were mirror images of Grace and Hank once upon a time. Back then, they thought the world revolved around them and nothing would ever tear them apart. They had imagined growing old together, celebrating all the gifts that life brought their way like the Robinsons were doing now.

Grace remembered Jake's college graduation. Her family had attended with her, but she'd kept thinking of Hank and how proud he would have been of their son. If things had been different and he hadn't been on the train that fateful day, she believed with all her heart that they would have had a good marriage.

Grace and Hank would have fought and made up over the years, but their marriage would have been filled with love and laughter. When they were still newlyweds, they had made plans and shared dreams. They'd wanted to travel after their children grew up and left home. Would they have been like the Robinsons? Still acting like newlyweds after all those years? Grace hoped so, but considering the man Hank appeared to be now, she wasn't sure.

She dug into her toolbox, then pulled out a Phillips-head screwdriver and stuck it into her back pocket. First, she had to scoot the dryer out so she could slip behind it and get to the vent hose. If she was lucky, it would be a simple clog. If not, she'd need to return to the Internet and troubleshoot.

As she worked, she thought about Lucinda, who'd known love and loss as Grace had. Well, almost. It was still surreal to realize that she was no longer a widow. Honestly, she didn't know what her title was these days. Until recently, Grace had been content with her life. She'd accepted Hank's death, and while she'd always mourn the loss, it didn't consume her life or define her anymore. And then she'd met Spencer.

The familiar *click-clack* of tiny nails alerted Grace that she was no longer alone. A cold nose nudged her bare ankle.

She smiled at her faithful dog. "What do you say? Is today the day when I solve the mystery of the non-drying dryer?"

Winston wagged his tail.

She was sure he was giving her a thumbs-up. "Okay, let's give it a try."

Before Grace could resume her work, the bell over the front door jingled.

Winston barked and ran for the laundry room door before stopping to glance back at her.

"Or maybe not. Let's go see who's here." Grace followed the dog to the foyer. She rounded the corner to find a tall, thin man in his midthirties.

Appearing a bit lost, the man ran his hands through his blond hair until it stood up in several places.

Winston bounded over to him and yipped.

The man bent down to pet the dog.

"That's Winston. He loves meeting new people. And I'm Grace Porter, one of the owners. Can I help you?"

The man straightened and looked at her. His light-brown eyes were full of pain. "I'm searching for Christie Thompson. Is she in?" His voice held a touch of a Southern accent.

The man's anguished expression made Grace think this was the reason Christie had been so quiet since her arrival. "We don't normally give out information on our guests. Are you a family member?"

"I'm her ex-boyfriend, but if she'll give me a chance I'd like to fix that." The man's frown slowly spread into a smile, lighting up his face and showing off twin dimples.

"She's not here right now. Would you like to leave her a note?" Grace hadn't gotten a chance to get much of a read on Christie yet, and she wondered what the young woman would think of her ex following her to Magnolia Harbor.

"No thank you. What I've got to say to her can't be said on paper. Plus, she'd just throw it away." He motioned toward Grace's hand. "What's with the screwdriver? Is something broken?"

Grace glanced down in surprise. She'd forgotten she was still holding the tool. Embarrassed at greeting a visitor that way, she slipped it into her pocket. "My dryer's not working, and I think the vent's clogged."

"I could check it out for you," he said.

"That won't be necessary," Grace said. "But I appreciate it."

He pulled a business card out of his wallet and handed it to her. "My apologies. I should have started out with an introduction. Blake Dalton from Matthews, North Carolina. I'm the owner of Dalton Fix It. I hope to become Christie's boyfriend again and maybe someday her husband."

She pocketed the card. "On second thought, I'd love to take you up on your kind offer." Given her lack of sleep, Grace didn't have the energy or patience to deal with the problem on her own.

"Let me get my toolbox." Blake walked out the door.

When Blake returned, Grace ushered him to the laundry room.

Winston trotted behind them and watched Blake as he began to work.

Grace stepped out of his way. "Normally, my sister and I do most of the repairs around here ourselves, but every now and then we come across something out of our league."

"I think that's great," Blake said. "Christie's very independent too. She can do pretty much anything she sets her mind to. She worked her way through school. Paid for the whole thing herself without any financial aid and graduated at the top of her class."

"That's impressive," Grace said.

He nodded. "She has a good heart too. You should see her with kids. She's a natural. I know she wants a houseful, which is fine with me. She's the best person I know. Way too good for me."

"I'm sure that's not true," Grace protested. "You seem like a great person. I mean, here you are helping me out, and I'm a complete stranger."

"Fixing things is what I'm good at."

"Then you should be able to fix what's going on with you and Christie, right?" Grace asked.

"I've tried," Blake admitted as he reached for the vent brush.

"First, you need to have confidence in yourself," she said. "You two have talked about your relationship. Do you know what the problem is?"

"Besides the fact that she knows what she wants and I'm thickheaded?" he asked with a grin. "In all seriousness, I know what the problem is, and I've learned my lesson. Now I need to figure out how to show her that I'm all in and convince her to give me a chance."

Grace could tell that Blake meant every word. This young man was head over heels in love. She couldn't stay silent and watch their love go down in flames. Normally it was Winnie who played matchmaker, but Grace felt the need to give it a try. "Would you mind if I made a few suggestions?"

"Not at all. I'd appreciate any advice you can give me."

"I'm sure the fact that you drove here to win Christie's heart will score a few points for you," she went on. "But you need to tell her the truth about how you feel. Grand gestures are nice, but nothing beats words straight from the heart."

"I'm ready to do that."

"She might not want to listen the first time you try or even the second, but don't give up," Grace told him. "If you love her, fight for her."

And didn't Hank deserve the same chance to fight for her?

Christie

The last several hours at the Heritage Library had been pure heaven for Christie as she read page after page of newspaper archives, losing herself in the past.

Of course, she might have made more progress on her genealogy project if she hadn't kept getting sidetracked, but she couldn't help the fact that she loved learning about history. Anyway, it didn't matter. She was on vacation, albeit a working one. It might take her all week to locate the information she was searching for, but in the end, she'd find what she needed.

She always did.

Christie's patience, persistence, and purpose had seen her through the teens and those tough, lean years as she worked her way through school. Those attributes had helped her rein in her impulsive side when so many of her classmates ran wild and got into trouble. And they had caused her to stick by Blake for three long years.

Maybe they hadn't been a blessing in that case.

But she didn't see anything wrong with being a hopeless romantic. Or rather a hopeful romantic as long as she was also realistic and knew when to call it quits.

Leaving Blake had broken Christie's heart, but they had different visions of the future. She desperately wanted a family of her own—before it was too late. He was basically a frat boy stuck in an adult body.

Okay, that wasn't fair. It was true that Blake was close to his buddies and they spent a lot of time together. And in all fairness, she spent a lot of time with her sister and friends, but she never put them before her relationship with Blake.

It was too bad he couldn't say the same thing.

Shaking off the grouchy mood that had settled over her, she returned the reference materials to Phyllis Gendel, the head librarian. "Thank you so much."

"Please let me know if there's anything else you need," Phyllis said. "I'll do some digging into James Frank Riley and see if I can discover anything."

Christie had told Phyllis all about her genealogy project, mentioning the name of the man she was hoping to locate. "I really appreciate it. I'll be back tomorrow." She left the library and walked to her car.

On the drive to the inn, Christie promised herself that she wouldn't think of Blake for the rest of her vacation. In fact, she'd use her time to focus on her genealogy project and spoil herself a little. Maybe there was a spa nearby. There was nothing like a good massage to chase the blues away.

Feeling better already, Christie parked her car, grabbed her bag, and jumped out, humming her favorite song.

"I must say that song really picked up my mood."

Christie startled at the voice. She hadn't even noticed a man standing on the front steps. He was older but quite good-looking with dark hair and amazing green eyes. He was tall and lanky, like a runner. While Blake was as tall as this guy, he was more muscular with broad shoulders, blond hair, and light-brown eyes. They were opposites in every way.

When Christie realized she was sizing the man up against her ex, she plastered on a smile and shoved all thoughts of Blake away. "It's nice to hear my singing makes someone smile. My sister tells me it chases the coyotes away."

He laughed. "Maybe I should talk to Grace and see if she'll add karaoke to hospitality hour. Then you could share your beautiful voice with all the guests."

Christie put a hand to her chest. The idea of singing in front of people scared the daylights out of her. "I'll have to pass."

"That's a shame. I'm Hank Porter, by the way."

"It's nice to meet you. I'm Christie Thompson." She assumed he was related to Grace since they had the same last name.

Before she could ask him about it, Winston bounded over to them, turned in a circle, and sat down.

Christie was shocked to see Blake behind the dog. "What are you doing here?"

"I went to your house," Blake said. "When you didn't answer the door, Mrs. Finklemeyer came out and told me where you were. She said you were with your new boyfriend." He glared at Hank.

Christie wasn't surprised that her neighbor had eavesdropped on her conversation with Carly and found out where she was going. Mrs. Finklemeyer was always sticking her nose in everyone else's business. But Christie was confused why the woman thought Christie had a new boyfriend. Christie would talk to her neighbor when she got home.

For now, she needed to find out why Blake drove almost four hours to find her. "Are you okay? Is there some kind of emergency?"

"No, I'm not okay," Blake answered. "But there's no emergency."

"Who's he?" Hank whispered to her.

"My *ex*-boyfriend," Christie said loud and clear. She glanced at Blake and watched his face crumple. Her heart ached at his reaction.

"Look, if you're stalking the lady, I'll call the police," Hank said.

"There's no need for that," Christie assured him. "If you could give us a few minutes, please?"

Hank nodded. "But I'm going to wait up here on the stairs to make sure you're all right."

Christie flashed Hank a small smile. She wanted to tell him that his concern was unnecessary, but at the same time she didn't want to cause a scene. Maybe if she let Blake think Hank was her new boyfriend he'd finally get the point and realize they were over. She sighed. Just seeing Blake broke her heart all over again.

"I'm not stalking Christie," Blake told Hank, "and I'd never hurt her."

"Really?" Hank asked, raising his eyebrows. "You showed up out of the blue, and it doesn't sound like she's thrilled to see you. Not to mention she said you're her ex."

Christie stepped between the two men and held up her hands. "Let's all take it down a notch. Hank, I appreciate your concern, but everything is fine. If you could excuse me for a moment."

Without another word, Hank climbed the steps and sat down on the porch.

Christie turned to Blake and gestured toward the parking lot. "I think you should leave."

"Give me ten minutes to explain," Blake said. "Please?"

"You've had plenty of chances," she reminded him. "In fact, you've had three years to prove you're ready for the next step in this relationship, but when the time came to step up, you stepped back. I appreciate the grand gesture of driving down here, but do me a favor and leave."

"Christie," he said in the tone that always tugged at her heart, "I love you."

Her eyes burned, and she wiped away the tears. She couldn't do this anymore. It hurt too much. "You need to go. You're only making this harder."

"Do you expect me to just let you walk away?" Blake asked. "I'm going to fight for us, and I won't give up. You love me, and I love you. We're good together. Give me another chance."

It took everything she had not to throw herself into his arms and agree. He was right—she did love him. If only he wanted marriage and children like she did. "We've been over this. You and I want different things from life and this relationship."

"We can work it out," he said.

"How?" Christie buried her face in her hands, then shook her head. "You know what? I'm not doing this again. You had your chance. It's over. I'm done. Go home." She spun around and bounded up the stairs with Winston on her heels.

Hank was waiting for her. "Are you okay?" he asked.

"Not really," she replied. "My head is pounding, and I could use some time alone."

"No worries. I'll catch up with you later." When Hank opened the door to the inn, Lucinda stood in the doorway. He held the door open for her, then went inside.

Lucinda approached Christie, and the two watched Blake slowly get into his truck and drive away.

"There's something about that one," Lucinda said, narrowing her eyes.

"Oh, that was my ex," Christie replied as she watched the truck disappear down the driveway.

"Not him." Lucinda motioned toward the house. "Hank."

"Why do you say that?" Christie asked.

Lucinda sat in one of the rockers. "He's some relation to the owner, but that's not it. Every time I see him he looks like he's up to something nefarious. If I were you, I'd watch out for him."

"I just met him," Christie said as she sat down beside her.

"Actually, he was very sweet. His relation to the owners might explain his protectiveness."

Winston curled up at their feet.

The door opened, and Grace stepped out with her purse over her shoulder and a list and car keys in her hand. She stopped when she noticed Christie and Lucinda. "Is everything okay? You both look upset."

Christie was more than upset. Not only was her head pounding, but her stomach threatened to revolt. Turning Blake away was the hardest thing she'd ever done. "My ex-boyfriend, Blake Dalton, found out I was here and followed."

Grace nodded. "We met earlier. He very kindly fixed my dryer and refused to let me pay him."

"That's Blake," Christie said. "If he thought you needed a shirt, he'd give you his." Blake's generosity was a blessing and a curse because he never thought about how today affected tomorrow, and she did constantly. "I guess he assumed I'd swoon when he arrived and forget all the problems that led to our breakup. Sadly, I don't think Blake Dalton of Dalton Fix It can fix our problem this time."

"It was a nice gesture," Lucinda said as she rocked and gazed across the lawn with a faraway look in her eyes. "My Charley was never one for big displays. Goodness knows that man couldn't take a hint if I hit him over the head with it, but he was good for the little stuff, and I knew his love was true."

"It sounds like you had a wonderful marriage," Grace commented.

"Oh, there were days when I wondered if he preferred the cows' company to mine. Truth be told, there were times I didn't mind, especially when the children got older." Lucinda folded her hands. "That man was far from perfect, and he could drive me nuts. But he was mine, and I loved him."

"I'm not searching for perfection," Christie said. "I only want commitment."

Grace frowned and sat down in the other chair. "I don't mean to pry, but isn't that why Blake was here?"

Christie blew out a frustrated breath. She'd had a great afternoon, but after the long drive and all her research compounded by Blake's appearance, she was suddenly drained. "Yes and no. He's perfectly happy with us dating indefinitely, but I want a more permanent type of commitment, the kind that comes with a ring and kids."

"When he lost you, perhaps Blake changed his mind about marriage and family," Lucinda suggested. "It might be worth it to give him another chance."

Christie stared toward the road, where she'd last seen Blake's truck. How could she take another chance on someone she knew would only break her heart again?

Grace

Tuesday morning after the guests had enjoyed breakfast in the dining room, Grace cleared the dishes and refreshed the suites while Winston supervised.

Once everything was tidied, Grace and Winston stopped by the kitchen, where Charlotte was removing a few ingredients from the refrigerator.

"There you are." Grace sat down at the island, anxious to update her sister. "I just got a message from Jake. He'll be here next Tuesday."

"That's great," Charlotte said, setting the ingredients on the counter. "I can't wait to see him."

"Me too. Do you have any errands you need to run this morning?"

"No. I was going to test out a couple of new recipes for my next book." Charlotte grabbed a few bottles from the spice rack. "Would you like to be my taste tester?"

"As long as you don't need my opinion right away." Grace wiped away nonexistent crumbs on the counter and gazed out the window at Lake Haven.

"It'll be a couple of hours minimum." Charlotte studied her sister. "Is everything okay?"

"Everything's fine," Grace said. "All the guests are out, so I refreshed the rooms under Winston's watchful eye."

The dog plopped down on the floor, put his head on his paws, and sighed.

Charlotte grinned. "It looks like you wore him out."

"I believe so," Grace said with a faint smile.

"What's Hank doing today?" Charlotte asked.

"He said he was going into town," Grace said. "So it would be a good time for me to slip away. Spencer got home late last night, and I need to tell him what's going on before he hears it through the grapevine."

"Agreed. Go ahead, and I'll hold down the fort." Charlotte smiled. "Maybe you and Spencer should take advantage of this beautiful day and spend it together."

"Thanks for understanding," Grace said. She got up and hugged her sister. "What would I do without you?"

"For one thing, you'd be doing a lot more cooking," Charlotte teased.

Grace laughed, then turned to Winston. "Would you like to go for a walk?"

The dog jumped up and ran to the back door, wagging his tail.

"I think that's a yes," Charlotte said.

"See you later." Grace grabbed Winston's leash, but she didn't bother clipping it on his collar because she knew the dog wouldn't take off.

The two of them walked out the door and headed toward Blossom Hill Farm, where Spencer lived. The small pecan farm was close to the inn, so there was no point in driving. Besides, she didn't want to take the chance that Hank might drive by and see her car parked in front of Spencer's house.

Not that she had anything to hide.

She hadn't done anything wrong, and she was not ashamed of her relationship with Spencer. They'd been friends for a long time before they'd gone on their first official date. Some would even say she'd taken things too slowly and needed to let go of the past. But her caution had more to do with the present than the past. Grace didn't want to rush their relationship because she was afraid of losing Spencer and his friendship. Thankfully, he was a very patient man.

As for the situation with Hank, she was trying to be considerate. While they hadn't discussed their future plans, Hank had made it clear that he had hopes of reconciling and picking up where they'd left off.

Grace honestly didn't know if that was possible. How could they simply resume their marriage after so many years had gone by? They weren't even the same people anymore. They had both aged and matured. She doubted that would have been a problem if they'd done it together, but after doing so apart, they were practically strangers. In fact, so much time had gone by that their baby was grown up. Jake had his own life.

And did she even want a relationship with Hank?

From what she'd seen so far, the years in Europe had drastically changed Hank Porter. He was no longer the easygoing, gentle man she'd fallen in love with. This new Hank looked like her Hank, but there was something about him that made her feel slightly unsettled and anxious. It seemed like her subconscious was trying to tell her something, but she wasn't willing to listen or couldn't hear the message.

Maybe Spencer could help her make sense of it.

As they approached the white farmhouse, Winston spotted Spencer's chocolate Lab, Bailey. Winston glanced at Grace, then ran ahead to play with his friend.

Spencer rounded the corner of the house, wearing work jeans, boots, and an old T-shirt covered in oil stains. A smile lit up his face when he saw her.

Grace returned the smile as she joined him.

"What a nice surprise." Spencer leaned down to kiss her cheek, careful not to get any of the dirt and oil on her. "I was just going inside to clean up and head over to see you."

"Great minds think alike," she said.

Together they walked to the front steps and took a seat so they could watch the dogs frolic in the yard.

"How was D.C. and your friend's retirement party?" Grace asked.

"It was good to catch up with friends," he answered. "Cam and his wife are excited about moving to Vermont to open a bed-and-breakfast. I also caught up with one of my former coworkers Quinton Danvers. He's thinking about putting in his papers and calling it quits."

"Wow," she said. "Big moves for both of them."

"They've served their country well. Cam was in for thirty years, and Quint's still a baby with only twenty years of service."

"Twenty years is a long time," Grace murmured.

"What's wrong?" Spencer asked. "You seem a little off today. I know I wasn't gone long, but I was hoping you'd be happier to see me." He shot her a playful grin and gently bumped her shoulder with his.

"It feels like you've been away for weeks. And of course I'm glad you're home. I missed you." Grace frowned. "But I don't know how happy you're going to be after I tell you my news."

"Whatever it is, it can't be that bad," he responded. "You know you can tell me anything."

Grace took a deep breath and plunged ahead. "As it turns out, I'm not a widow after all."

"What does that mean?" Spencer grinned. "Did you get married while I was away?"

"Believe it or not, that would be less strange," Grace told him.

"So what happened?"

"This is so complicated," she said with a groan. "On Sunday, I had a surprise guest show up—my dead husband, Hank."

"How can that be possible?" Spencer asked. "I think you're being scammed."

"No, it's him."

"I'm sure it looks and even sounds like him. But I've seen this kind of thing before. Scam artists are great actors. Plus, it's been a long time since you've seen him, so it's easier to explain any differences as changes."

"That's not what this is," Grace insisted. "He's simply an older version of Hank. And he knows things only Hank would know. I realize it sounds preposterous, but he survived the train crash and now he's back."

"If he survived, then where has he been for the last two decades while you've mourned his loss and raised Jake on your own?" Spencer asked, his normally calm voice dropping in volume.

Grace had seen Spencer upset before, but this was something else. "Why don't we go inside and talk?" she suggested. "But first, I want to tell you again that I missed you and I'm so glad you're home."

Spencer hugged her, and she didn't even care if he got dirt and grease on her clothes. It felt wonderful to feel his strong, warm arms around her. With him by her side, she knew she could figure out this mess.

Spencer whistled, and both dogs came running.

They all filed into his farmhouse. The dogs plopped down on the floor in the living room.

"Would you like a cup of coffee?" Spencer asked.

"Sounds great." Grace followed him to the kitchen. She spied a bakery box on the counter and peeked inside to find a cherry pie. "Are you saving the dessert for another time?"

"I picked it up in hopes of sharing it with you," he said. "Would you mind getting a knife, plates, and forks?"

She smiled as she retrieved the items, enjoying the normalcy of the moment.

Spencer poured cups of coffee while Grace sliced two generous pieces of pie and set them on plates. Not for the first time, she noted what a good team they made.

"Want to take this out to the back deck?" Spencer asked.

"That sounds perfect. Then Winston and Bailey can play if they've got any energy left."

They walked outside and sat at a small table. It was set up under an umbrella on the deck to protect them from the afternoon sun, but the May heat still beat down around them, stealing what little energy she had. Or maybe that was due to the lack of sleep and the constant battle on her nerves.

As Spencer ate his pie, she related Hank's story of the train crash and how he'd rebuilt his life.

Spencer—patient, intelligent, insightful—said nothing.

"And that's it," Grace said. "Until last week, Hank didn't remember his real name, his life with Jake and me. Nothing. He thought he was Gustav Heinz. I know it sounds unbelievable."

"It sounds something all right." He set his empty plate aside and eyed her uneaten slice. "Can I get you something else?"

"No thanks." Grace slid her plate toward him. "I haven't had much of an appetite the last couple of days."

Spencer began eating the pie. "All he had on him on the train was a ticket with the name *Gustav Heinz*? No identification? Passport? Driver's license?"

"No, I guess all those documents were in his suitcase," she said. "But his suitcase was lost in the crash."

"That doesn't sound right. Most men leave their wallets in their pants pockets. They don't carry them in a briefcase or a carry-on bag."

Grace thought about that for a moment. Spencer made a good point. She didn't remember ever seeing Hank put his wallet in his briefcase before. "Maybe he felt it was safer there for some reason."

"It would be easier to steal his suitcase or carry-on bag than to pick his pocket," Spencer pointed out. "Also, I've never seen a train ticket with the passenger's name printed on it."

That surprised her. "Isn't it like an airplane ticket where you have to give your name and date of birth?"

"I'm going to regret that later." Spencer pushed the second empty pie plate away and rubbed his stomach. "As for the ticket, no. You can walk up to the counter and buy a seat on any train. The conductors onboard check passports randomly, but most of the time, you can move between countries in the European Union without presenting your passport."

"That seems convenient if you're fleeing from the law."

"It's a lot like traveling between the States here," he said. "Except in some cases they're stricter and you never know when you're going to be asked to show your passport. And there's one other thing that doesn't make sense."

"Only one?" Grace massaged her temples.

He gave her a sympathetic smile. "Hank had an American accent."

She'd wondered about that too. Hank was good at languages, but his native tongue should have given him away. "I'm curious about something else. I know Hank spoke German, but even with the trauma and head injury, wouldn't his thoughts have been in English?"

"That's a good question. I'm not an expert on amnesia, although I have a few contacts I can ask."

"Like your friend Quinton with the bureau?" she asked.

"Among others."

Grace rested her hand on Spencer's arm and leaned forward. "You're right that some things don't add up about his story. While I want answers, I don't want to cause Hank any more grief. He's been through so much. Don't forget that he lost the chance to see his son grow up. Those are years and memories he can never get back."

"I'm not trying to take him away from Jake," he said. "I just want to make sure he's really Hank Porter. Keeping you safe is my top priority."

She inhaled and looked away, wondering if she should share her other concerns with Spencer. Or should she wait until she'd had time to talk with her lawyer? In a way, it felt disloyal discussing her marriage and husband with another man. But honestly, Grace didn't even know if she was still married to Hank.

Normally, she would discuss the situation with her sister and aunt, but she was finding it difficult to talk to them about it. Grace knew they were struggling to deal with Hank's reappearance, and she didn't want to tell Charlotte about the disparaging comments Hank had made about the inn. Grace knew it would set off her sister's temper, but she didn't blame Charlotte. She was angry about it too.

The previous night during hospitality hour Grace had overheard Hank tell Lucinda that if it were up to him he'd modernize the whole inn. He'd start by changing the room names to numbers, and then he'd gut all the suites and replace everything with modern, streamlined furniture.

Hank had added that no one wanted to stay in an outdated antebellum mansion built in 1816 that was located in a small town. People preferred to book rooms in hotels in the middle of major cities so they could be steps away from the excitement of nonstop nightlife.

In other words, not the Magnolia Harbor Inn cliental.

"What is it?" Spencer asked, jolting her out of her thoughts.

"The whole situation has been overwhelming to say the least," Grace answered. "I have all these questions running through my head and so many conflicted emotions. At times, I'm not sure if I'm coming or going. That's a new feeling for me."

"What can I do to help?" Spencer asked quietly.

"For now, I want you to be my sounding board and give me some time to figure this out," she answered. "I need to see my lawyer. After all, Hank was legally declared dead, so I don't even know if we're still married. And there's the insurance company to notify."

"How is Jake handling the news?"

"I don't know," Grace said. "He can't come home until next week because of his work schedule."

"That might be better for him. He'll have more time to adjust to the idea, rather than getting thrown into it like you were. And it'll be good for you to see him in person."

"It will," Grace agreed. "But on top of all this personal stuff, we have an inn full of guests." She dropped her head into her hands, wishing the pounding at her temples would go away.

"Hey, it's going to be all right," Spencer assured her. "You're not alone. You've got Charlotte and Winnie to help you with the inn and the guests, and I'm here for whatever you need of me."

"You're being awfully nice considering I just told you that you're the other man in my life now," Grace said with a small chuckle.

"Is that part of what's bothering you?" Spencer asked, obviously surprised. "Do you feel like you're cheating on Hank with me?"

"We did take vows." Even if they were a lifetime ago. Even if she'd thought she was a widow for most of that lifetime. And even if she felt as though she'd given those promises to a completely different man than the one who had shown up on her doorstep.

Regardless, Grace couldn't ignore the commitment she'd made to Hank. Until the attorney confirmed it, she wasn't a widow anymore, so she wasn't free to date Spencer.

"Those vows included the words *until death do us part*," Spencer reminded her, "and he was declared dead. I think you might find that your vows are no longer binding."

Grace nodded, knowing she needed to talk to her attorney. She had to learn about her options. It was terrible feeling powerless. But she wanted to get a better grasp on her emotions first.

Was Spencer right about their vows? And did she want him to be?

Christie

As promised, Christie returned to the Heritage Library. This time, Lucinda accompanied her.

When they walked into the library, Phyllis smiled at them from behind the reception desk. "I found something that might be useful to you," she said.

"Really?" Christie asked. "What did you find?"

"A possible relative of James Frank Riley," Phyllis replied. "His name is Stephen Riley."

"That's wonderful," Christie said. "Did you learn anything else about him?"

"I certainly did," Phyllis said. "Stephen and his wife, Amelia, live on a farm about fifteen miles from Magnolia Harbor."

"I can't believe you made such an incredible discovery," Christie said. "Thank you."

"It was my pleasure," Phyllis said. "I enjoyed it."

"Do you think we can stop by and talk to Stephen and Amelia?" Christie asked.

"I don't see why not." Phyllis jotted down an address on a slip of paper, then gave it to Christie.

"Do you want to take a drive?" Christie asked Lucinda.

"Let's go," Lucinda said.

After thanking Phyllis again, Christie and Lucinda hurried out to the car and headed to the farm.

Christie felt a shiver of anticipation when they arrived at their destination. She drove around the circular driveway and parked.

When Christie got out of the car, she paused to glance around the farm. Three red barns stood near the white two-story farmhouse, and a windmill turned slowly in the slight breeze. It was so peaceful.

"Are you ready?" Lucinda asked, joining her.

Christie led the way to the front door, then rang the bell and waited.

A moment later, a dark-haired woman opened the door. "May I help you?"

Christie introduced herself and Lucinda and summarized her genealogy project. She explained that Phyllis had discovered that Stephen Riley might be related to James Frank Riley.

"I'm Amelia, Stephen's wife. Stephen isn't here, but maybe I can shed some light on a few things. Please come in." She ushered them into a cozy living room. "Have a seat while I get some snacks."

Christie and Lucinda sat down on the sofa.

Amelia reentered the room, carrying a tray laden with glasses of lemonade, a plate of oatmeal cookies, and napkins. She set the tray on the coffee table. "Don't be shy. Help yourselves."

Christie and Lucinda thanked their gracious hostess as they retrieved their drinks and cookies.

Amelia took a seat in the armchair across from them. "Phyllis was correct. Stephen is James Frank Riley's great-nephew. He had a younger brother named Euen. Euen's son, Ian, is Stephen's father."

"My client is Jean Johnson," Christie said. "She's the daughter of Estella Johnson, née Riley, daughter of James Frank Riley."

"If you'd like, you can take a peek at the family Bible and some photo albums," Amelia offered. She retrieved the Bible and several albums from a cabinet and stacked them on an end table.

Christie got up and flipped through one of the photo albums.

"This is wonderful. Would you mind if I took a few pictures to show Jean?"

"Not at all," Amelia replied as she sat down.

Christie snapped some pictures, then closed the books and rejoined Lucinda on the sofa.

"So how did you find out about the family connection in South Carolina?" Amelia asked.

"Good old-fashioned sleuthing," Christie replied. "And maybe a little Irish luck."

The women laughed.

"We found Jean's mother's birth certificate in a trunk in her attic," Christie said. "It was buried under a pile of clothes and newspapers. The clippings were from an old newspaper in Magnolia Harbor and listed James Riley, which was also Jean's grandfather's name, but that's all I had to go on. I still don't have much else, like why her mother doesn't have one single picture of her parents."

"I can tell you that," Amelia said. "There was a rift in my husband's family. They're as stubborn as they come."

"What happened?" Christie asked, taking another cookie.

"Back then, James was something of an important man," Amelia said. "He had this farm, the lot next door, and some others. Plus, he was a lawyer. James raised his children with certain expectations, and he wanted more for them and their families."

"There's nothing wrong with wanting the best for those you love," Lucinda said, then took a sip of lemonade.

"No, there isn't," Amelia said. "But James didn't care about love. He only cared about money and status. When Estella fell in love with Albert, a man James didn't approve of, he forbade his daughter from seeing him again."

"What did Estella do?" Christie asked.

"As you can imagine, that didn't fly with her," Amelia said. "One night when her parents were out to dinner, she packed up a few things and ran away with Albert."

Christie gaped at her. It was like something out of a romantic movie.

"A few years later, Estella's mother died from cancer," Amelia continued.

"How terrible that she never got to see her daughter again," Lucinda said.

"Rumor has it that she'd seen Estella in secret several times before she died," Amelia said.

"That's quite a story," Christie said.

Amelia nodded. "Thankfully, the rest of the men in the family are nothing like James."

"Families can be so complicated," Christie said, toying with her napkin. "But isn't it better having a family than being alone?"

"It depends. I don't think it's better if family means living without love." Amelia took one of the photo albums and opened it. She showed them a picture of two teenagers laughing. "That's me and Stephen when we first met in high school. He still makes me laugh."

"He seems like a wonderful man," Lucinda said.

"He is, but there was a time when my mother urged me to pick someone else," Amelia admitted.

Christie and Lucinda glanced at each other. Christie was curious about Amelia's comment, but she didn't want to pry into the woman's private life.

"Oh, it's common knowledge," Amelia said. "Stephen got hurt playing sports in school and can't father children. I'd always pictured a houseful of them. I had to decide between a marriage with love or one with kids."

"Life is all about sacrifices," Lucinda said. "Look at Estella. She had to give up her family to be with Albert."

"Sometimes a sacrifice is more of a compromise," Amelia said. "Stephen and I weren't able to have our own biological children, but we became foster parents and eventually adopted two kids. So it all worked out for the best."

Christie wondered if she loved Blake enough to sacrifice her dreams of a family of her own. She shook her head. It didn't matter because Blake didn't want to commit in a permanent way, and she wasn't willing to compromise and be his girlfriend forever.

"Jean said she had a wonderful childhood," Christie said. "So it sounds like Estella made the right choice, especially if she still saw her mother in secret."

"I know that Stephen and the rest of the family would love to meet Jean," Amelia said. "Please let her know that she's welcome here anytime."

"She'll be delighted," Christie said. "Thank you."

"In fact, she should join us next month when we celebrate Stephen's birthday," Amelia added.

"I'll let her know," Christie promised.

"Well, you ladies are welcome to keep making copies of these old pictures," Amelia said. "But I've got pies to bake for our church dinner tomorrow night."

They thanked Amelia for her hospitality again, and she retreated to the kitchen.

Christie took some more pictures of the photo albums. "Thank you for coming out here with me today," she told Lucinda.

"It's my pleasure," Lucinda said. "Besides, this is exciting. It's like solving a mystery."

"I don't know if I'd go that far," Christie said with a grin. Filling in this family tree hadn't even been along the same lines as solving a good Nancy Drew mystery, but she understood what her new friend meant. Normally, it took a lot more digging to find all the missing pieces for her genealogy projects.

"Will your client be surprised?" Lucinda asked.

"I'm sure she will be," Christie answered. "I know she'll also be thrilled to finally know more about her ancestors and where they came from. I can't wait to tell her that she has family down here who want to meet her."

"Couldn't she ask her parents?"

"Sadly, they both passed away when Jean was in college," Christie said. "Her grandparents were already gone by then, and she didn't have any siblings. Neither of her parents talked about their extended family, so she's been on her own for years."

"Well, that's a shame," Lucinda remarked. "Even when I was mad at my sister or brother growing up, I was glad to have them around, and my four children are as thick as thieves." She smiled. "Much to my dismay at times."

Christie laughed. "I believe my mother feels the same way about me and my sister."

"So what are you going to do now?" Lucinda asked.

Christie snapped another picture. "I'm not compromising."

"I was referring to your next steps in the genealogy project," Lucinda said, raising an eyebrow.

"Oh, I'm sorry," Christie said. "I guess my mind is on Blake."

"What aren't you going to compromise about?" Lucinda asked. "Has he asked you to marry him?"

"No, he hasn't," Christie answered. "And that's the problem. I want to get married and start a family."

"How long have you two been going steady?"

She didn't have the heart to tell her new friend that no one called it *going steady* these days. "We've been dating for three years."

"And you don't think he's serious when he's stuck around for that amount of time?" Lucinda asked.

"No, I don't. I think I'm more like a habit he can't break. Or an old, familiar blanket he doesn't want to throw away because then he'd have to get used to a new one."

"From the way that man looked at you, I think you're a lot more than a worn-in blanket to him," Lucinda said, a twinkle in her eyes.

Christie didn't reply. Instead, she took a few more pictures, returned the albums to the stack, and covered the cookie plate. "We should probably get out of Amelia's way."

They stopped by the kitchen and said goodbye to their hostess, then headed toward the car.

As they drove to the inn, they continued their conversation about Blake.

"Don't get me wrong," Christie said. "Blake is an incredible guy. But he wants to have his cake and eat it too, and he thinks the party should never end. I like to hang out with friends as much as anyone else, but I want a family of my own. Quiet nights. Sleepy, lazy Saturday mornings with just the two of us doing stuff on our own at home. Those things drive Blake crazy."

"So it's your way or the highway?" Lucinda asked.

Christie laughed, unsure if she should be insulted or not. "Well, for the past three years I tried it his way, and I was—"

"Miserable?" Lucinda interrupted.

"Not miserable but not really happy either." Christie turned down the drive to the inn and parked under a shady tree. "I felt like something was missing from my life. The sad part is that I do love him. If I thought someday he'd be ready and if I had the luxury of time on my side, I'd wait for him. But he's never going to want what I do, so there's no point in dragging this relationship on any longer."

They got out of the car and crossed the lawn to the front porch.

Lucinda stopped and rested a hand on Christie's arm. "He might surprise you. I have a feeling you made that young man take a long, hard look at his life and really see what was important to him. You should at least hear him out."

"I'll think about it," Christie promised as they climbed the steps and walked through the front door.

"I'm glad to hear it," Lucinda said.

Pushing away thoughts of Blake, Christie reflected on their successful excursion. Now that her project was finished, the rest of her trip was strictly a vacation. "I don't have to do any more research tomorrow. Would you like to go sightseeing in Charleston with me?"

"I'd love to," Lucinda said.

"Great. I'll ask Grace and Charlotte for some suggestions on where to go," Christie said. "In the meantime, I need to upload all the pictures I took at Amelia's and update my client." She also needed to call her sister to tell her the good news.

"Of course," Lucinda said. "I think I'll relax on the veranda for a while."

Christie went upstairs. The first thing that hit her as she entered her suite was the scent of roses. Sitting on the nightstand was a huge bouquet of long-stem red roses.

As she walked closer, she noticed a small card tucked in between the blooms. She plucked out the card and read it.

Christie,

I'm sorry. Please have dinner with me so we can talk.

I love you.

Blake

She dropped down onto the armchair and groaned. How was she supposed to stay strong and hold her ground when Blake was doing things like this? The man was definitely wearing her down. Maybe she should agree to hear him out and get it over with. Then she could send him home and be done with it. But she knew that wasn't going to happen so easily.

Christie had repeatedly told Blake that it was over, and he clearly wasn't listening. He was a great guy, but he was stubborn. Still, if she didn't talk to him, she'd never get to enjoy the rest of her vacation.

Sighing, Christie glanced around the room. It was spotless. Clearly, Grace or Charlotte had cleaned up. But her laptop had been moved from the dresser to the bed, and the dresser drawers weren't closed all the way.

Chills ran down Christie's spine. The innkeepers would never leave the dresser drawers partially open. And why would they move her laptop? She wondered if Blake had delivered the flowers to her suite himself. Had her door been locked? Now she couldn't remember.

She rushed over to the dresser and opened each drawer. Nothing seemed to be missing, but her clothes had been moved around. It appeared that someone had been searching for something. She checked the closet as well, but she didn't notice anything unusual.

Christie closed and locked her door and headed downstairs to find the innkeepers. Lost in her thoughts, she didn't see Hank until she ran into him.

He was holding a small jeweler's bag, and the impact sent it flying.

"I'm so sorry." Christie picked up the bag and handed it to him. "I didn't hurt you, did I?"

"I'm fine, but are you okay?" Hank studied her face. "You seem upset."

"I'm all right," she said. "I need to find Grace and Charlotte."

"I think they're on the back veranda," Hank said. "Is there anything I can do to help? You know, I'm sort of one of the owners here."

"No thank you," Christie said. "I just need to ask them about the flowers that were delivered to my room."

"Ah yes, from your ex-boyfriend," Hank said. "It sounds like he's trying to win you back."

Christie felt uncomfortable. She didn't want to talk about Blake to a man she didn't even know. "Please excuse me." She headed toward the veranda.

Laughter confirmed Hank's guess, and she followed the delightful noise to find Grace, Charlotte, their aunt Winnie, and Lucinda sitting on the veranda. Winston was sprawled out at Grace's feet.

The women warmly welcomed Christie, and Winston bounded over to her.

"Come join us for some sweet tea," Charlotte said.

"Thank you." Christie took a seat.

Winston jumped onto her lap and curled up.

Charlotte poured a glass and set it down next to Christie. "You're just in time to sample my new lemon profiteroles."

"Lemon?" Christie asked. "I thought profiteroles were filled with cream or sometimes ice cream. I've never heard of them with any other kind of filling."

Charlotte placed a profiterole on a plate and gave it to Christie. "Tell me what you think."

Christie bit into it and savored the sweet yet tangy filling. "Oh, this is perfect on a hot day like today. Are these for your new cookbook?"

"Maybe. I might save them for the inn." Charlotte grinned. "You know, keep a few family secrets."

"Speaking of family secrets, we heard you had a lot of success in your genealogy project today," Grace said. "Congratulations."

"Thanks. Phyllis's help was invaluable," Christie said. "When I went up to my room to e-mail my client an update, I noticed the roses from Blake."

"The flowers are gorgeous," Grace said.

"I don't remember the last time Dean sent me flowers. Probably the last time we argued." Charlotte laughed. "No, that's not true. Sometimes he surprises me with a bouquet."

"Your uncle likes to surprise me with them too," Winnie said.

"Buck brought me cheerful daisies when he asked me to dinner," Lucinda remarked.

Christie realized this was the first time Lucinda had mentioned a man other than her late husband. "Did you say yes?"

Lucinda shook her head.

"Why didn't you go?" Winnie asked gently.

"My children would have been upset if I'd gone on a date with another man," Lucinda answered. "Besides, I couldn't do that to Charley."

"But you mentioned that it's been three years since Charley passed," Grace said. "It wouldn't make you unfaithful if you went to dinner with Buck."

"I'm sure Charley wouldn't want you to be alone," Charlotte said.

"Girls, everyone heals on their own time." Winnie reached over and patted Lucinda's hand. "When you're ready, you'll know."

Lucinda smiled at them with a gleam of tears in her eyes. "Thank you all."

The women sat in silence for a few minutes as they sipped their tea and gazed at Lake Haven.

Lucinda broke the silence. "Are you going to give that young man another chance?" she asked Christie.

"I don't know," Christie admitted. "I was considering it, but then it appeared that someone had been snooping around in my room. Did Blake deliver the flowers himself?"

"No, I took them," Charlotte said.

"We'd never let another person in a guest's room," Grace added.

"Did you happen to move my laptop when you were cleaning this morning?" Christie asked. "Or open the dresser drawers?"

"Of course not," Charlotte said. "I lifted the computer to dust under it, but I left it where it was. We never open the dresser drawers or the closet when a guest is occupying a room."

"Can you tell us exactly what made you feel like someone had gone through your room?" Grace asked.

Christie filled them in on how she'd found the laptop in a different place from where she'd left it and the dresser drawers partially open with her clothing moved around.

"When I dropped off the bouquet, the door was locked, and the drawers were fully closed," Charlotte said. "The room was as neat as a pin from when it had been cleaned."

"This doesn't make any sense," Grace said with a frown. "No one else has keys to the rooms. Nothing was missing, correct?"

"Not that I could see," Christie said.

"What about your room?" Grace asked Lucinda. "Did it look like anyone had gone through it?"

"I haven't been upstairs yet. I came straight out here." Lucinda gave Christie a concerned look. "Why in the world would your ex-boyfriend want to snoop through your room? What could he possibly gain from it?"

"Nothing that I can see." Christie paused as she considered it. "My nosy neighbor at home told him I was here with a new boyfriend, but I have no idea where she got that idea. Maybe Blake was trying to see if I was sharing a room with this new guy. After yesterday's encounter, I'm afraid he thinks I'm seeing Hank."

"Hank? Oh my, but he's old enough to be your . . . well, much older uncle." Grace laughed and shook her head. "I hope Hank didn't encourage the idea."

"He kind of did." Christie took another bite of profiterole. It had been hours since breakfast, and she'd eaten only a couple of oatmeal cookies at Amelia's. Plus, when Christie got stressed, she ate sweets. At the moment, she could eat the whole plate of lemon puffs.

"I'm so sorry," Grace said. "That's the last thing you needed."

"You can't control what others do," Winnie reminded her niece.

"She's right," Christie said. "Hank thought he was helping me. In fact, it was rather gentlemanly of him."

"Still, we try not to create drama for our guests," Grace said. "Please accept our apologies."

"Don't worry about it," Christie said.

"As to your room, I can't imagine what happened," Grace said. "We don't have security cameras because we value our guests' privacy, and I'm sure Blake never went upstairs."

Maybe Christie had been mistaken. After all, it would be totally out of character for Blake to break into her room and snoop around. He had high morals. "Unless something else happens, why don't we forget about it? As I said, nothing was taken, so I probably overreacted. It could be nerves from traveling alone. Or the creepy thriller I was reading before I went to bed last night."

"Are you sure?" Grace asked.

The other women regarded Christie with concern.

"Yes, I'm positive," Christie said with more confidence than she felt.

"Then let's get back to those flowers," Lucinda said. "Are you going to give that young man another chance?"

"Well, let's see what he does next." Christie grinned. "He's made me wait on him for years, so I can't make it too easy for him."

9

Grace

After breakfast the next morning, Grace left Charlotte and Winnie to handle the rooms and drove into town to run a few errands.

She parked her Honda CR-V on Main Street and scanned her list. It wasn't too bad. If she hurried, she could return to the inn before lunchtime and finish some of her other chores there.

As she stepped out of her car, she heard someone call her name. She turned to see Police Captain Keith Daley hustling toward her.

"I'm glad I caught you," the captain said. He removed a handkerchief from his pocket and wiped the light sheen of sweat that glistened on his bald head.

"Oh?" Grace asked. "Is there something I can do for you?"

"I wanted to talk to you about what happened at the inn," he said.

Grace wondered if Christie had reported the incident with her room yesterday. Then it hit her. "You mean Hank's return? It has been a shock."

"I'm sure," Daley said. "I heard he's had amnesia all this time. I can't imagine not knowing who I was for all those years, not to mention missing out on watching my sons grow up. Such a shame."

"Yes, it is," Grace said, "but he's excited to get to know Jake now."

He nodded. "Did Jake come home?"

"Unfortunately, he's in the middle of a big project, so he hasn't been able to get away from work," she explained. "But I expect him on Tuesday."

"That's good. A son should know his father." The captain scratched his chin. "Where did Hank live all this time? Was it in Prague?"

"No, he was staying in Vienna, Austria," Grace answered. "And working as a waiter."

"What a change of pace from being an engineer," Daley said, eyes wide. "It must have been hard for Hank with no family or friends around and not being fluent in the language."

Grace agreed that it was a difficult situation to imagine. But was the captain simply curious about Hank's life for the past two decades, or was it something more? After all, Daley was first and foremost a cop, and he took his job of protecting the residents of Magnolia Harbor to heart. However, this was Hank they were talking about. Her husband. Well, maybe. But a man she knew and the father of her child.

"Actually, Hank speaks German fluently, so that must have helped," Grace said. "Still, it couldn't have been easy for him. He didn't realize he had a family who was searching for him, and he didn't even know his own name."

"What name did Hank go by?" he asked.

"Gustav Heinz."

The captain raised his brows.

Grace laughed. "I can already tell what your next question is. You need to work on your poker face."

Daley laughed too. "So, how did Hank get that particular name?"

Grace proceeded to explain what had happened to Hank. She concluded with how he had finally remembered her and Jake.

"That's an incredible story," he said.

She nodded and decided to change the subject. "So, how's Helen?" The captain's wife was a good friend who suffered from rheumatoid arthritis, and Grace admired the fact that Helen never let the disease get her down.

"She's having a good day today. Thanks for asking." He checked his watch. "I need to get going. Take care."

After Daley walked away, Grace strolled down the street to Spool & Thread to talk to Judith Mason, who owned the fabric shop.

Judith was busy ringing up a customer, so Grace wandered around the store, admiring the many finished projects and beautiful materials as she waited.

As Judith finished with her customer, Grace approached the counter.

"Thank you." Judith handed a bag to her customer. "Remember you're always welcome to join The Busy Bees here on Tuesday nights at six for quilting and socializing."

Judith was the leader of The Busy Bees quilting group that met at the fabric shop. Winnie and Helen Daley were two regular members.

"I'll try to stop by." The woman thanked Judith and left.

Judith greeted Grace warmly. "So what brings you in today?"

"I wanted to check on the quilt for the church fundraiser," Grace said. "I know we have more than a week until the big day, but I was hoping if it was done, we could put it up for preview to get everyone excited."

"Oh, that's a good idea, but it's not quite ready. I'll give you a call as soon as it's finished."

"That would be great. Thank you."

"I heard you've had some excitement of your own this week," Judith said. Her dark-brown eyes gleamed behind her glasses. "That must have been something else, opening the door and seeing your dead husband standing there."

Grace laughed at Judith's phrasing. "It was quite a shock."

"Could you tell it was Hank right away?" Judith asked. "Did he sweep you into his arms and tell you how much he still loved you?" She laughed. "Listen to me going on and on. That's what I get for watching all those old romance movies."

If only it had been like an old romance movie. Grace didn't want to talk about Hank anymore. There were too many mixed feelings and questions racing through her mind. Even though Judith's questions weren't offensive, they could lead to deeper territory. "There's nothing wrong with romantic daydreaming when you've got time. As for me, I have a to-do list a mile long and not nearly enough hours in the day."

"I know what you mean," Judith said. "I'll let you get going."

"Thanks," Grace said, then sailed out the door.

Her next stop was the newspaper office, but Grace's energy level called for coffee, so she decided to pop over to the Dragonfly Coffee Shop for a latte. Maybe she'd even treat herself to a cookie too.

As Grace entered the coffee shop, she heard someone calling her name again. She turned to see Patty Duncan, another member of The Busy Bees. Suddenly, Grace wished she had sent Charlotte on these errands and stayed at the inn instead. She didn't have the time or energy to entertain the Magnolia Harbor gossip mill, no matter how well-intentioned.

"What a surprise seeing you here in the middle of the day," Grace said, taking her place at the end of the line. "Did they switch your schedule at the hospital?"

Patty followed. "Oh no, I'm on an early lunch break and thought I'd grab some goodies for our little troupers."

"That's so thoughtful of you." Grace knew that being a pediatric physical therapist couldn't be easy, but Patty had a caring heart, and it seemed to be the perfect job for her. "Thank you again for the church fundraiser donation. The tickets to the play will be a huge hit. I plan to bid on those myself."

"You're welcome. Will you be taking Hank?"

"We'll see," Grace said. She was startled by the question, but she guessed she shouldn't have been. Hank had mentioned he planned to go to town. Apparently everyone knew their story now.

Patty put her hand over her heart. "It's so romantic how he's never stopped loving you all these years and how he knew there was something missing from his life, even when the poor dear couldn't remember his own name."

"Yes, I suppose it is."

"It's like something from a movie that Billy auditioned for recently," Patty said, referring to her son. He was always close to landing his big break in Hollywood. "He's hoping to get called back on the lead role. Fingers crossed."

"Wow, that's fabulous," Grace said. "I'll definitely keep him in my thoughts."

Angel Diaz, the youngest member of The Busy Bees, was working behind the counter. After finishing with a customer, she motioned to Grace. "You're next."

"It was good to see you," Grace said to Patty. "Keep me in the loop on whether Billy gets his callback."

"I will," Patty said. "Talk to you later."

"What can I get you today?" Angel asked.

Grace gave Angel her order, then retreated to a corner table. She hoped no one else would spot her and want to talk about Hank. It was understandable that his return was huge news. Magnolia Harbor was a small and quiet town. It was exactly the way Grace liked it.

But she didn't want to be the center of attention. She preferred her life to remain calm, orderly, and free of drama. That had all changed when Hank strolled through the door of the inn. Now Grace's life was upside down, and she had no idea how to right it.

When Angel called out her order, Grace hurried to the counter to retrieve it.

Instead of staying, Grace took her latte and cookie to go. It was a gorgeous day with blue skies, and the humidity hadn't quite kicked in yet. She waved to a few people as she walked to her next destination. Across the street, she spotted Joel and Felicity sitting on a park bench. The honeymooners were snuggled together, sipping coffee and sharing a muffin.

Grace was overcome with mixed emotions. She was truly happy for Joel and Felicity. They were a great couple and madly in love with each other. She wished them a long life of beautiful moments that they would always cherish.

But she couldn't stop the dark, heavy sadness that wrapped itself around her. Joel and Felicity reminded her so much of her and Hank all those years ago.

As Grace continued walking, she thrust the negative emotions away. They wouldn't do her any good.

When she arrived at the *Harbor Gazette* newspaper office, she approached the woman sitting behind the front desk.

"How may I help you?" the woman asked.

"I'd like to place an announcement for the Fellowship Christian Church's upcoming fundraiser," Grace said.

The woman picked up an electronic tablet. "You're Grace Porter, owner of the Magnolia Harbor Inn, right?"

Grace smiled. "Yes, my sister and I own it. Have you ever been there?"

She shook her head. "Are you the one whose husband reappeared after being presumed dead for more than twenty years?"

"Yes, I am," Grace said, wishing once again that she had sent Charlotte on these errands. "Is there a form I need to fill out for the announcement?"

The woman waved the electronic tablet at her. "We'd like to do a story on your husband, his life in Europe, and your romantic reunion."

Grace didn't know that she'd call it a *romantic* reunion. She could think of many other ways to describe how she felt when Hank had appeared—shocked, bewildered, jolted, and even angry. She hadn't been swept off her feet. Instead, she'd been blown away by the bombshell dropped on her.

"You'd have to speak with Mr. Porter and see if he's willing to give an interview," Grace said. She didn't want to be rude, but she had other things to do, and talking to everyone in town about Hank wasn't on her list.

"Could I get Mr. Porter's phone number?" the woman asked.

Grace realized she didn't have his number, but she wasn't going to admit that to this woman. It struck her as odd that Hank hadn't given it to her. Then again, she hadn't shared her number with him either.

"If you'll give me your card, I'll have him call you if he's agreeable," Grace replied. "In the meantime, I need to place that announcement for the church."

"Of course." The woman handed Grace a business card, then retrieved a form from a file cabinet and passed it to her.

While Grace filled out the form, the woman attempted to wheedle personal information out of her, but Grace ignored it.

Grace finished the form, thanked the woman, and returned to her car.

As she drove back to the inn, she considered the story request. She planned to discuss it with Hank, but first she'd talk to Charlotte. They appreciated publicity for the inn, but this might not be the right kind. And until Grace and Hank figured out and settled their relationship, she'd rather keep what was going on between them private.

Grace had been putting off the call to her attorney until she had a better grasp on her emotions, but she realized she needed to stop procrastinating and set up an appointment. She needed to know if she was still married to Hank. Did he have a claim to the inn? Did she need to pay the insurance company back?

But beyond the legal issues, she needed to figure out her head—and most importantly, her heart.

Grace

For a moment, when Grace saw the man sitting on the front veranda, happiness filled her heart. *Jake came home early*, she thought.

Then reality set in, filling her with confusion and uneasiness as she studied her husband. From a distance, he resembled Hank, but the question remained unanswered. Was he the same man she'd once loved?

She got out of her car and climbed the steps to the veranda.

Hank stood and scowled at her. "Where have you been? I've been waiting for you for hours."

Shocked by his sharp tone, she stepped back. "I'm sorry. Did you need something? I was out running errands, but Charlotte's here. She would have helped you with whatever you needed."

"I sincerely doubt that," he muttered through clenched teeth.

"What? Is everything okay?" Grace glanced at the front door. Did Hank and Charlotte have an argument? Even though Hank was technically a guest, she was more concerned about Charlotte.

"Yes, it's fine," Hank said. "I meant that only you could help me."

"So what do you need?"

"Are you free tonight?" he asked.

"Yes."

"Great. Then we can have dinner and talk. I'd say it's past time we got to know each other again. I'll see you at six." Hank leaned in and kissed her hand, then loped down the stairs to his car and left.

Grace stared after him as she collapsed into one of the chairs. She didn't remember Hank being so crafty. But she supposed if he'd asked her outright to dinner she would have found an excuse, as she'd been finding reasons to avoid him since he arrived.

She sighed. It was unlike her to dodge a problem. Not that Hank was a problem per se. The situation was the problem, and Grace didn't like trying to resolve an issue without being prepared. She needed to do research.

Of course, part of that research required her to have a heart-to-heart talk with Hank, and that wasn't going to happen if she kept avoiding him. At least dinner would give her a chance to get some of her questions answered. Every time someone asked her about Hank's life in Europe, something deep inside told her the story didn't quite add up.

A now-familiar truck pulled into the parking area, and Blake got out.

Grace smiled. "Good afternoon."

Blake waved. "How's the dryer holding up?" He stopped at the base of the steps and leaned forward to rest his arm on the banister.

"Like new," she answered. "I can't thank you enough."

He shrugged. "It was no big deal."

"Can I offer you a glass of sweet tea and a chair out of the sun?" Grace asked. "I'm sure Charlotte has some cookies or scones in the kitchen if you're hungry."

"No thanks," Blake said. He scanned the area. "I was hoping Christie might be around, but I don't see her car."

"She and another guest went sightseeing. You're welcome to wait for her." Grace wished these two would talk and find some middle ground. They were both such wonderful people, and she could see that they cared deeply for each other.

"I don't think she liked the roses yesterday," Blake remarked. "I called and sent her a few texts, but she didn't reply. I've tried everything to make her see that I'm serious."

"It sounds like she might need more time," Grace said gently. "I need to ask you a question about yesterday. Did you go into Christie's suite after you dropped off the flowers?"

"Of course not," Blake said, obviously startled. "I don't even know which room is hers. Plus, I don't have a key. And as much as I'm trying to change it, we're not together, and I don't belong in her space." He frowned. "Why would you ask me that?"

Grace regretted that her question had left Blake feeling perplexed and concerned. He clenched his fists and glanced at the front door. It was written all over his face that he wanted to check on Christie, but he knew he had no right. Grace's heart went out to him. "It's okay. I was just asking."

"No, you wouldn't ask without a reason," he said. "Is Christie all right?"

She let out a deep breath. "Yes, Christie is fine. But she thought someone was in her room and searched through her belongings. Please understand that I had to ask, because Christie's safety is a priority."

"She thinks I broke into her room?" Blake asked. "So that's why she wouldn't take my call or return my texts. I would never betray your kindness, and I know that is not the way to win Christie back. If there's anything I can do to help, please say the word."

"Thank you," Grace said. "I'll be sure to let you know—"

The sound of barking cut her off as Winston rounded the corner at a full run.

"Winston, come here," Grace said.

The dog kept running.

Grace flew down the steps after him. "Winston, stop!" She turned to Blake. "I don't know what has gotten into that dog."

"Looks like he's on the scent of something," he said. "I'll help you find him."

The two of them took off in pursuit, which led them around the far end of the inn, past Charlotte's cottage and into the woods. Both Grace and Blake called for Winston, but he didn't come. Thank goodness he kept barking.

Finally, they found the dog tangled up in a bush. He was covered in mud.

"Oh, Winston, were you chasing a squirrel?" Grace asked as she tried to free her dog from the bush. "You're filthy. What am I going to do with you?"

In response, Winston whined and hung his head as low as the tangled branches would let him. The poor dog's long fur was caught, and he couldn't get loose.

"I'll be right back," Blake said, then disappeared in the direction they'd come.

"It's okay, boy. We'll get you untangled in no time," Grace said, trying to keep Winston calm.

Blake returned with pruning shears. He'd changed into an old shirt, and he wore work gloves. "Give me a minute, and I'll get him loose. Once I get him free, I'll clean him up for you."

"I can't ask you to do that," Grace said.

"You're not asking. I'm offering," Blake clarified as he started cutting away the branches. "You've got an inn full of guests and no time to deal with this mess. Besides, it's a hot day, and Winston and I could use a little cooling off."

"Thank you so much," Grace said, marveling at his kind and considerate offer. She planned to put in a very good word on his behalf to Christie. Blake certainly deserved it.

He cut the last branch and gently freed the dog.

Winston yipped and wagged his tail, then plopped down in front of his rescuer.

Blake laughed and scratched behind the dog's ears.

Winston led the way to the inn.

In the side yard, Grace set up the kiddie pool she sometimes bathed Winston in during the warmer months. She left her dog in Blake's capable hands and went inside. What she needed after the bizarre day she'd had was a nice glass of sweet tea and a few moments with her sister.

After being away from the inn all morning, Grace stopped by the front desk to check for any messages or calls that she might need to return. They were booked solid for the next few months with summer, but Grace hated to make people wait for her to call them back.

Grace didn't have any messages, so she called her attorney's office. The receptionist informed her that he was on vacation, so Grace scheduled an appointment for the following week. She hung up, relieved that she would soon be able to discuss the matter with him.

The bell above the front door chimed. She glanced up to see Monty and Jamie. Both were a little flushed from the heat, but their bright smiles told Grace they'd had a wonderful day.

"Can I interest either of you in something cold to drink?" Grace asked. "You might like to relax on the veranda. It's nicely shaded this time of day."

"Oh, that sounds perfect," Jamie said. "I don't suppose you have any of those iced raspberry cookies left, do you? Those were so good last night, and we skipped lunch."

"If I'd known she was going to starve me today, I would have had another waffle at breakfast," Monty teased. "Or at least taken my son up on his offer for a slice of cake at the reception we attended." He laughed as he patted his stomach. "Not that I need it."

Jamie shook her head and smiled. "I wish I could eat like you. You eat all the carbs you want and never gain a pound."

"You need to figure out what your secret is and share it with the rest of us," Grace said to Monty. "You could be the most popular man in the world if you did."

"Our son is the same way," Jamie told her. "That boy lives on junk food—pizza, burgers, fries, ice cream—and he's a beanpole. It's not right."

Grace laughed. Only a mother could be so honest. "I know what you mean. My son is built like a runner, and I'm sure he's never had to think twice about what he eats."

"Does your son live around here?" Jamie asked.

"No, he's in Raleigh," Grace said. "He's a software programmer. Whenever he talks to me about work, I'm lost. It's amazing what he does."

"I'd be right there with you if our son had gone the tech path," Jamie said. "But he majored in music therapy. Thankfully, music is my passion, even if I can't sing to save my life."

Grace and the Robinsons continued to talk about their sons, how they were as babies and toddlers, and all the way up to the men they had become. They told stories about the years of playing T-ball, Little League, flag football, and soccer. They discussed last-minute science projects, book reports, and cupcakes for class parties. Things that drove them crazy, sent them to bed exhausted, and moments they wouldn't have missed for anything in the world.

Moments Hank had never been able to experience. Important snippets of life had been stolen from him through a freak accident, but Grace reminded herself that it could have been much worse.

Grace promised to bring the cold drinks and cookies out to the veranda for the Robinsons in a few minutes and headed to the kitchen.

As she prepared a tray, thoughts swirled in her head, making her feel a little dizzy. She sat down at the island to regain control.

Charlotte entered the kitchen. Her expression turned to concern when she saw her sister. "Are you all right?"

"I believe so," Grace said. "It's been a busy morning, and I didn't have lunch."

"Let me get you something to eat," Charlotte offered.

"I need to prepare a tray for Jamie and Monty first," Grace said. "I promised them your iced raspberry cookies and something cold to drink." She started to stand up.

But Charlotte stopped her sister by putting a hand on her shoulder. "You sit. I've got this. I made some fruit-infused water this morning that will be a perfect complement to the cookies. There's also some chicken salad in the fridge. Maybe I should include that along with fresh sliced Italian bread. I think you could use a little protein too."

"Thanks. That sounds wonderful." Grace sat there for a few quiet moments while Charlotte prepped her lunch and the tray.

Charlotte set a plate in front of Grace. "Don't move until every bite is gone."

"Thanks," Grace said. "They're waiting on the veranda."

"I'll be right back." Charlotte took the tray out to their guests.

When Charlotte returned, she made her own plate, then sat down and joined her sister.

Grace took a bite of the creamy chicken salad with bits of cranberry and walnut. "It's delicious."

"I'm glad you like it," Charlotte said. She scooped up a spoonful of salad and spread it across a slice of bread. "Did you get all your errands done?"

"Yes, but I regretted not asking you to do them," Grace admitted.

"Why?" Charlotte asked.

"Everyone asked about Hank." Grace described the conversations she'd had in town and explained that the *Harbor Gazette* requested a story about Hank. "I wanted to talk to you about it before mentioning it to him."

"I appreciate that," Charlotte said. "Let me mull it over for a bit."

"So, how did it go here?" Grace asked. "Any problems?"

Charlotte shook her head. "Winnie and I turned out the rooms in record time."

"Good. Did our other guests feel like their rooms had been searched?"

"No, and from what I could tell, nothing is missing either," Charlotte said. "So maybe Christie was right when she said she might have been mistaken or it was a case of nerves from traveling alone."

"Hopefully that's all it was," Grace said. "I talked to Blake about it."

"What did he say?"

"He swears he didn't go into her room."

"Do you believe him?" Charlotte asked.

"Yes, I do." Grace took a sip of her water. "By the way, Blake's outside giving Winston a bath."

Charlotte raised her brows. "Why?"

"Winston chased something—most likely a squirrel," Grace answered. "When we found him, he was covered in mud and tangled up in a bush."

"Oh no. Poor Winston. What was that dog thinking?" Charlotte chuckled. "I'll have to make a treat for him and something special for Blake to thank him."

"Oh, I have a dinner date tonight," Grace said, remembering. "Well, dinner plans anyway."

"I can handle the hospitality hour on my own," Charlotte said. "Where are you and Spencer going?" She ate the last bite of her sandwich.

"I'm having dinner with Hank."

Charlotte started coughing. Her face turned red, and her eyes started to water.

Grace jumped up and refilled her sister's glass.

Charlotte sipped until the cough subsided. "Thank you." She narrowed her eyes. "Did you say you're going on a date with Hank?"

Grace sat down and pushed her empty plate away. "It's not really a date. Hank asked me to have dinner, and I agreed because we need to talk. I have so many questions for him. When he showed up, I was too flabbergasted to take it all in and process it."

"It's completely understandable." Charlotte reached out to hold her hand. "How are you feeling now?"

Grace sighed. "Confused. Conflicted. Like my life is out of my control."

"And I know how much you hate that." Charlotte smirked, then turned serious. "Are you still in love with Hank?"

Grace would always love Hank Porter, the man she married, the father of her son, but she wasn't sure if she was still in love with him. "I don't really know him anymore. He's lived almost as long as Gustav as he did as Hank, and Vienna is a lot different than South Carolina."

"That's true."

"I used to know his favorite dish was pulled pork with corn bread and peach cobbler for dessert. I have no idea what it is now." Grace threw her hands up. "I don't even know his cell phone number."

"You don't have to know someone's favorite food or phone number to love them," Charlotte said.

Before Grace could respond, the back door opened, and their aunt breezed in. "Good afternoon. How are we doing?" Winnie stopped when she noticed Grace. "What's wrong?" She hurried around the island and wrapped Grace in a warm, tight embrace.

"We're talking about Hank," Charlotte said, then filled Winnie in on their conversation.

Winnie pulled up a chair and poured herself a glass of fruit-infused water. She took Grace's hand. "No one said you have to figure this all out in a day or two. I know you came to terms with losing Hank a long time ago, so this is a lot to deal with."

Grace nodded, struggling to get her emotions under control. "I have to think of more than just me."

"No you don't," Charlotte protested.

Grace held up her hand. "Hear me out. There are legal issues I need to consider. Right now, I don't even know if I'm still married. If so, does Hank have a claim to the inn?" She glanced at her sister. "The answer to that affects both of us."

Charlotte sat back, clearly stunned. "I hadn't even thought of that."

"Have you spoken to your attorney yet?" Winnie asked.

"He's on vacation, so I can't meet with him until next week," Grace replied. "I also need to consider Jake and his feelings. I'm sure he's struggling with his father's sudden reappearance."

"Yes, it must be very difficult for him," Winnie said.

Grace took a deep breath and let it out slowly. "And then there's Spencer. I don't want to lose his friendship."

"You won't," Charlotte assured her. "Spencer would never hurt you."

"I don't know if I'm still in love with Hank," Grace admitted. "He's a complete stranger to me now. But I can't ignore the vows I made to him. I need to get to know him and see if he's still the man I married, the one I promised to love until death do us part."

No matter where that leaves me with Spencer.

Christie

After several hours sightseeing in Charleston, Christie and Lucinda returned to the inn.

"Thanks again for inviting me along," Lucinda said as she exited the car. "I had a wonderful time."

Christie slid out of the driver's seat. "I did too."

They walked across the lawn and climbed the porch steps.

Lucinda opened the front door and glanced over her shoulder. "Are you coming?"

"You go on ahead," Christie said. "I think I'll sit out here for a few minutes."

Lucinda nodded, then entered the inn.

Christie leaned against the railing, then was startled by the sound of splashing water. She followed the sound and spotted Winston bounding around a kiddie pool. Blake was standing next to him with a bottle of shampoo. His shirt was soaked.

Christie descended the steps and strode over to Blake. "What are you doing?"

"Giving Winston a bath," Blake said.

"I can see that," Christie said. "But why?"

Winston took that moment to shake sudsy water over the two of them and bark.

"Hello to you too, Winston," Christie said. "How did you get so dirty?"

"He was chasing something through the yard," Blake said. "Then he got caught in a bush. After I cut away the branches and set him free, I offered to give him a bath for Grace."

"Do you realize you're soaked?" She had to bite down on her bottom lip to keep from laughing as Winston pranced out of Blake's reach and shook again. The dog was having a grand time.

"Yeah, but I don't have an inn full of guests," he replied, "and I can throw this stuff in the washer back at my room."

"That was really nice of you," Christie said, touched by Blake's thoughtfulness. "Do you want some help?"

"No thanks. I don't want you to ruin your dress." Blake caught her eye. "You look really pretty today. You always do, but I like the way the purple brings out your hazel eyes."

"Thank you," Christie said. She should walk away, but she'd promised her sister when they were texting earlier that she'd give him a chance to talk.

"I heard you went sightseeing," Blake said. "Did you have a good time?"

"Is that your way of asking who I went with?" Christie crossed her arms and glanced away. This would never work between them.

"Nope. It's none of my business who you were with. I was just asking if you had a good time. I still like to know when you're happy."

"Yes, I had a good time," Christie said, softening a bit. "And I went with my new friend Lucinda."

He reached for the hose with one hand and tried to hold Winston with the other, but the dog moved in closer and started licking his chin.

Christie laughed. "Hang on." She kicked off her shoes and set her purse out of the way, then reached for the hose. "You need more hands for this little guy because he's too smart. Let me rinse while you work the soap out."

"Sounds like a plan."

As Christie and Blake worked together, she felt the tension between them ease.

"I heard about someone snooping around your room," he said. "You have to know I'd never invade your privacy like that. I want to talk to you, not spy on you."

He was right. She knew that wasn't Blake's style. She was ashamed to have even considered he'd do something so low and immoral. "I know. I was just upset. Please forgive me."

"It bothers me that someone was in your room," Blake said. "Do you think they were trying to access your computer for personal information or see if you had any small valuables that they could easily take?"

Christie shrugged. "Nothing is missing, and my computer is secured with a password that I'm pretty sure even a professional hacker couldn't guess."

"You mean it's not the name of your first pet?" he joked.

She laughed. "Not even close."

Winston suddenly made a break for freedom. Blake attempted to grab him, but the dog evaded him again.

Christie raced around the pool to block the dog's escape. But Winston jumped around, barking in glee, and she ended up covered in more suds.

"How did the person get into my room?" she continued. "Who besides Grace and Charlotte have a key?"

"What about your new boyfriend?" Blake asked.

Christie didn't know whether to laugh or sigh. "He's not my boyfriend."

"He's not?" Blake asked, obviously surprised.

"No, he's almost old enough to be my father. Or rather an uncle. He's a guest here. I think he's the owner's husband. It's kind of a complicated story from what I'm hearing. Either way, I don't think he'd snoop in my room or even have access."

Winston sat in front of Blake and wagged his tail as if saying, "I'll be good now."

Blake dived at him, but the dog danced away at the last second, and Blake fell flat on his face.

Christie burst out laughing as Winston climbed onto Blake's back and sat down. He was king of the mountain.

After coaxing Winston to get down, Blake held on to the dog by the collar. She turned the hose on, and he worked the suds out of Winston's long fur.

"It was probably my overactive imagination," she went on. "I was reading a scary thriller before bed."

Blake picked up a clean, wet dog and wrapped him in a towel. "I hope that's all it was, but you have good instincts, and I think you should listen to them. If anything else happens, you need to let the police know. Anyone could sneak in here."

"I will," she promised.

They sat down in a couple of Adirondack chairs while Blake toweled off the dog.

When Blake was done, Winston curled up on Blake's lap and fell asleep.

Christie grinned. "You wore him out."

"I think so," Blake said as he glanced down at the dog. He turned to Christie. "Did you at least like the flowers?"

"The roses are beautiful," she said. "I planned to call you today to thank you, but now I can say it in person."

Blake reached out as if to take her hand but stopped. "You deserve flowers every day."

"It's a thoughtful gesture, but I don't need flowers every day. Besides, it's even better when they show up at random times simply because the person was thinking of you."

"That's one of the things that makes you so special," he said. "You're not into material things. You don't shop for designer stuff, and your closet isn't overflowing with clothes you never wear. You don't want to go to five-star restaurants where you walk away hungry. You're all about the experience. I love that about you."

"Thanks, but there are things I want in life." Christie let out a deep breath, tired of having the same conversation with him and knowing he wasn't listening. "Let's not talk about us again, okay?"

"Fine, but I'm not giving up on our relationship."

Instead of responding, Christie changed the subject. "Do you have a softball game this week?" She tried to keep her tone light, but her stomach burned with a bit of resentment. The time he spent with his friends and how he put them first was a major contention between them.

"Yeah, but I'll probably skip it."

"How will the guys get along without their star first baseman?" she asked, startled.

He shrugged. "We've got second-string players they can pull from. They deserve some field time. Besides, it's only a game. You're more important."

Christie studied the man next to her. He wouldn't have given her that answer a month or two ago. If he had, they would still be together. "Well, I wish them good luck."

"How's your genealogy project going?"

Christie told Blake how the town librarian had discovered an obscure reference to her client's mother and from there led her to living relatives who confirmed the whole family tree and broke the scandal wide open.

As she delved into the details, Blake asked questions and paid attention, something he hadn't always done. Normally, he wasn't interested in the past and didn't think very much about the future.

Today she seemed to be seeing a whole new Blake. He still had all the admirable qualities of the man she'd fallen for over the past three years, but he held some promise too.

"They do Civil War reenactments nearby," he said. "You and your friend Lucinda should check them out. I was thinking I might go watch. It sounds interesting."

"But don't you have to get back to work?" she asked.

He shook his head.

"Who's taking care of business for Dalton Fix It? You told me you were completely booked." Christie wouldn't put it past Blake to have canceled all his appointments without considering how it would affect his bottom line. The guy never thought of the future.

"I promoted Sam to assistant manager, so he's running the show this week. He's doing great too. He's working on a few new marketing ideas for us."

"That's wonderful," she said. "Sam deserves it."

"We even hired a new guy. I didn't think we could afford it, but Sam showed me how adding another employee could up our game and cut my hours." Blake gave her a bit of a smug smile and settled deeper into his chair. "I'm actually on vacation this week."

Christie gaped at him. This was not her Blake. Not the guy who lived in the moment. Not the guy who only cared that today was covered and tomorrow hadn't arrived, so there was no use worrying about it.

This might be the man of her dreams.

Maybe it was the shock talking or the adorable way Blake sat there with Winston on his lap, but relaxing with him at the lake felt like living a dream. But she was afraid she'd wake up any second and find out reality hadn't changed.

Christie pushed her thoughts away. "That's great news. I'm happy for Sam and for you. What are you going to do with your time off?"

"I have to return to work by Saturday, but until then I thought I'd stick around here. Maybe watch that reenactment, check out Charleston, or spend the day kayaking." Blake gave her a small, hopeful smile. "I'd love it if you joined me."

Christie wanted to take him up on the invitation. She'd love nothing more than to spend the rest of her vacation with Blake doing fun things together as a couple. But although it seemed like he'd turned a corner, she still had her doubts. After all, a leopard didn't change its spots overnight, even if it had the best of intentions.

She closed her eyes, enjoying the sun on her face and the sound of birds serenading them from a nearby tree. There was something about Blake that made her feel safe, relaxed, and content. She hadn't been sleeping well since they'd broken up, but she could have easily fallen asleep right now in his calming presence.

"Penny for your thoughts?" Blake asked.

"They're not worth much right now." She smiled and reached over to scratch Winston's ears. "I feel like him, sleepy and relaxed. Too bad I left my book in my room."

"Is that all?" he asked.

"Isn't that enough?" Christie asked. "It's nice to stop and enjoy the moment. Being with someone who makes you laugh or experiencing something new with a friend. Those are the kind of memories I want to have when I'm ninety-five and zipping around a retirement home in my wheelchair."

"I can see you competing in wheelchair races."

They laughed.

"I heard that *Mamma Mia!* is coming to Charlotte in a couple of months," Blake said out of the blue. "Haven't you always wanted to see that play?"

Christie spun toward him as shock and happiness surged through her. "I have. Oh, I love that movie." She dropped her face into her hands and chuckled. "I'd be the worst audience member, singing along, probably dancing in my seat." Then she sighed.

"What's wrong?" he asked. "I thought that would make you happy."

"Carly hates that play, and I don't have anyone else to see it with. I'd feel weird going by myself."

"I'd go with you." Blake met her gaze, and Christie noticed sincerity in his eyes.

"You wouldn't feel weird going to a girlie musical?" she asked.

"Of course not. I'd go anywhere with you."

Maybe Christie should give him another chance or at least the opportunity to talk about their relationship and where it was going. If the man she'd spent the last hour with was any indication of who Blake truly was, then she owed it to herself and to him to see if there was any hope for a future.

Before she could respond, Grace approached them. "There you are. I was searching for Winston to make sure he hadn't gotten into any more trouble." She smiled as she took the now clean, dry dog and snuggled him.

"He was no trouble at all," Blake said, winking at Christie.

"Thanks again for freeing him from the bush and giving him a bath," Grace said. "I really appreciate it."

"It was my pleasure," he said.

"Please tell me you'll stay for our hospitality hour tonight," Grace told him. "Charlotte is making something special to thank you for all your help."

"Can you ask Charlotte for a rain check?" Christie asked Grace. "Blake and I are going out tonight."

From Blake's shocked but ecstatic smile, she knew she'd said the right thing.

Grace

"Are you sure you wouldn't rather go out to dinner with Hank instead of eating here?" Charlotte opened the refrigerator and retrieved the canapés she'd made earlier. She set them on the center island and headed toward the pantry. "What if I have to refill a platter or something?"

Grace popped the pan of corn bread into the oven and set the timer. "Then you'll come in and get it. This is my life. He may as well see what it's like. I know how the old Hank handled chaos, but I need to see how this new version does."

"Are you sure you're not choosing to stay here because it's your territory?" Charlotte asked, raising her brows.

As Grace considered her sister's question, she bit into one of the cream puffs Charlotte was serving this evening. Their guests were in for a treat. Shrimp ensconced in cream cheese with fresh chives and chopped mushrooms nestled in the center of the buttery pastry.

"Being here feels right. It's home, so I'll be more secure and confident, but there are also no prying eyes and every ear isn't tuned into our conversation. This whole thing between Hank and me is awkward enough without the whole town getting involved. Plus, it's not fair of me to leave you alone on such short notice. If you need me, I'm here."

Charlotte leaned against the island, her arms crossed in front of her. "You do remember I used to run one of the most prestigious kitchens in Charleston, right? I think I can handle a handful of guests by myself."

"Yes, I remember." Grace hugged her sister. "But just in case you need me, I'm here, and just in case I need you—"

"I'm here." Charlotte wrapped her arms around Grace and rested her head on her shoulder for a moment.

As the two sisters worked in tandem, one cooking dinner for two and the other preparing appetizers and desserts for their guests, they talked about plans for the summer and upcoming events.

"How's the cookbook coming along? Will those shrimp cream puffs be included?" Grace popped another one into her mouth, not caring if they ruined her appetite for dinner. She was a fair cook, but she couldn't hold a candle to her sister.

Charlotte grinned. "By that look of delight on your face, I'm guessing they should be."

"Definitely," Grace said.

"Would you like me to set aside a few for you and Hank?" Charlotte asked, reaching for a small serving plate.

Grace shook her head. "Save them for the rest of the guests. Hank was never big on shrimp."

"What are you making for dessert?" Charlotte's face scrunched up in horror. "Please don't tell me you're doing fried cheesecake. My poor kitchen will need a deep cleaning in the morning to get the smell of grease out."

Grace laughed. "Don't worry. I'm making peach cobbler."

"Thank goodness," Charlotte said. "Okay, I'm going to set up the veranda, but let me know if you need any help."

Grace waved Charlotte off and returned to her cooking. She wanted to get everything done before Hank arrived so they'd have room to sit at the island. She'd thought about having dinner in the formal dining room, but with an inn full of guests, they still wouldn't have any privacy to talk. The only other option was to eat in her quarters, but that felt like too much privacy. She didn't want to give Hank the idea that he was once again welcome in her space.

Tonight was about the two of them getting to know each other again. Sort of a second first date.

Charlotte sailed in and out of the kitchen, taking the food and wine out to the veranda, as Grace set the plates on the island and cleaned up.

After Charlotte finished ferrying the food to the veranda, she set a small vase of flowers and a votive candle in the center of the island. "Just a little something to help you relax. Considering it's the kitchen, it still looks lovely, but it smells divine too, which is probably even better."

"Thank you," Grace said, lighting the candle.

"Feel free to save me some food. Or not." Charlotte grinned as she headed out the door.

A few seconds later, a knock sounded on the door.

Grace waited for the door to open. When it remained closed, she was impressed. It seemed that Hank had taken her comment about boundaries seriously. She opened the door.

Hank smiled and handed her a large bouquet of stargazer lilies. "You look lovely as always. Thanks for agreeing to have dinner with me."

"Thank you." Heat stole up her cheeks. Grace was glad she had taken a few minutes to freshen up and change out of her jeans and cotton top into a light linen dress. It wasn't anything fancy, but she loved the bright red fabric, and she supposed the sleeveless style showed off her arms. "Make yourself comfortable while I put these in water." She reached for a vase on top of the fridge.

Before she could grab it, Hank took the vase down and handed it to her.

"Thanks." She smiled and stepped back, putting space between them. "I hope you don't mind eating in. With a full house, I didn't want to dump all the work on Charlotte tonight. It may not seem like it, but running the inn is a lot of work."

"I've noticed. Actually, I've noticed that you never stop working. This place is too big for only two people. You need to hire help."

Grace set the vase of flowers on the counter. She'd put them in the living room later where everyone could enjoy their lovely scent. "Charlotte and I are fine on our own. When we need help, Winnie lends a hand, and we have someone who maintains the grounds for us. Occasionally we hire temporary help."

"Still, you should be able to enjoy a night out," Hank said.

"I do, but I need more than a few hours' notice," Grace said, then changed the subject. "I hope you're hungry because I made your favorite dishes. Or rather, what used to be your favorites. I don't even know if you still like pulled pork, corn bread, and peach cobbler. If not, we could join the rest of the guests for the amazing appetizers Charlotte made."

Hank grinned and rubbed his hands together. "Are you kidding? I've been dreaming of Southern food for weeks. One of the first things I did was eat a fried catfish sandwich. I didn't even wait until I left the airport. I'd been craving one for so long that I didn't care that it was subpar food."

"It's a good thing we live in South Carolina," Grace said lightly, trying to ignore Hank's comment. But it sounded like he'd been craving Southern food even before he'd remembered where he was from, and that bothered her.

"Is there anything I can do?" Hank glanced around the kitchen, appearing lost, but that was nothing new. Even before, he'd never been much help with the cooking.

Grace smiled and shook her head. "Just sit, eat, and enjoy."

Hank complied, taking a seat at the island.

She pulled out the dishes of pulled pork, corn bread, and peach cobbler from the warming oven and set them on the island, where she already had the condiments and coleslaw, along with a salad and some fresh fruit to balance the meal. Everything she remembered Hank had loved before.

Hank dug into his food. "This is fabulous. You didn't have to go to so much work for me. Next time, I'll make sure to give you plenty of notice so I can take you somewhere nice."

He continued eating, evidently oblivious to the insult he'd dealt with his words. The Magnolia Harbor Inn might not serve dinner, but it had a solid five-star rating from its guests and Charlotte was an incredible chef. Granted, Charlotte hadn't cooked dinner for them, but Spencer had never complained about Grace's cooking.

Grace shoved the hurt feelings away and focused on the goal for the night—getting to know Hank again. "How does it feel to be home?"

"It's good but strange," Hank answered. "After living in Vienna for so long, the South seems very slow. And Magnolia Harbor is much smaller than Charleston. There's nothing going on."

"There's certainly a relaxed pace here," she said diplomatically.

"I was talking to Gus the other day, and I forgot how slow people from the South talk," he continued. "Or I guess I'd just gotten used to how fast Europeans talk. Either way, it took everything I had not to tell him to spit it out already."

"Patience was never your strong suit. You'll have to work on that," Grace said, snapping back. Hank's comment about her uncle stung, and it was out of character for the man she used to know. She'd been trying to cut Hank some slack and be understanding, but it was getting harder.

They ate in silence for a few minutes.

"Did you ride one of those scooters in Vienna?" Grace asked, veering the conversation to a lighter subject. "The kind they always show in the movies." She smiled as she imagined Hank zipping over cobblestone streets on a Vespa.

"Of course not," Hank replied. "I wouldn't be caught dead on one of those things. I had a sleek convertible."

"On a waiter's salary?" she asked. "You must have worked in a very high-end restaurant."

"I did, but I got lucky and found an older model that had low miles," Hank said. "The owner had recently bought it and barely had a chance to drive it before he passed away. His widow didn't like driving, so the car had been sitting in her garage for several years when I spotted it. She had no idea it was a collector's edition and was glad to get rid of it. Too many memories for her." He smiled. "A win for both of us that day."

Grace wasn't sure she'd agree. It sounded more like Hank had taken advantage of the widow. "It's a shame you couldn't bring the car with you." She pushed the food around on her plate. Her stomach was in knots, and she wasn't able to eat more than a few bites.

"The car's in storage," he said. "When the time's right, I'll have it shipped here. A friend of mine will handle the details of sending my stuff over when I'm ready."

Grace thought for a moment about how expensive it must be to ship a car from Europe. Hank must have done well for himself as a waiter.

Hank took another helping of the pulled pork. "Tell me about Jake."

"What would you like to know?"

"What was he like growing up?" he asked. "Was he a good kid?"

"Jake was a great kid," Grace responded, a sense of pride settling over her. "Since he was a child, he's been compassionate, smart, and inquisitive. He's always been interested in how things work."

"Did he play sports?"

"He ran cross-country in high school and college," she said. "Are you nervous about meeting him?"

"A little," Hank admitted. "What if he doesn't like me?"

"Why would you think that?" Grace asked.

"Unlike you, I wasn't there for Jake when he was growing up," he said. "I don't have the right to expect unconditional love from him. He's a man now, and he's able to form his own opinions."

"You don't have to worry about Jake," she assured him. "Your son is a wonderful person, and you'll be so proud of him. He's become everything we'd ever hoped. He has a kind heart, and he's always giving of himself to others."

"It sounds like you did a great job raising him," Hank said, reaching out to hold Grace's hand.

She gently pulled it away and took a sip of her wine. "I did my best, but he made it easy. I think it's because we gave him such a solid, loving foundation to start with."

"Maybe you're right, but I'm still a little nervous."

"It might be a bit awkward when you first see him, but give him five minutes and I'm sure you two will hit it off." Grace smiled. "Hopefully, you'll understand his tech speak better than I do. He's intelligent, and he likes sharing what he's doing at work."

"What kind of job does he have?" Hank asked.

"He's a software programmer."

"I always told you that computers were the wave of the future." He glanced around the room. "Speaking of the future, you should think about modernizing this place. Maybe replacing those old-fashioned keys with key cards and setting up automatic room checkout to give you more free time."

Grace laughed and rolled her eyes. "Electronic door locks aren't very antebellum. I think we'll leave the inn as it is, but thank you for the suggestions. Did any of the hotels in Vienna retain their old-world flair? Or are all they all modernized now?"

"Most are modernized," he said. "At least the upscale ones that are worth staying at. Guests might choose to stay in a place that resembles a castle, but they still want modern amenities."

The door opened, and Charlotte walked into the kitchen with a tray full of empty dishes. She smiled but didn't say anything.

"Do you need a hand?" Grace jumped up from her chair to help her sister.

"No, I've got it. You two enjoy your dinner." Charlotte quickly unloaded the tray, then went to the refrigerator to get more appetizers and another pitcher of sweet tea.

"Is everything going okay?" Grace asked.

Charlotte nodded. "The Robinsons and Bensons are chatting with Lucinda on the veranda. It's such a lovely night, and they're all relaxing and nibbling on the snacks."

"That's good," Grace said. "I'm glad they're enjoying themselves."

"The Robinsons are tired and didn't feel like going out to dinner, and the Bensons have a late reservation at The Tidewater," Charlotte continued. "So I thought I'd double up on the food to help tide them over."

"What about Lucinda?" Grace asked. "Does she have plans tonight?"

"She might be waiting for Christie to get back from her coffee date with Blake," Charlotte replied. "She didn't say, and I haven't asked her. If it looks like she's on her own, I might invite her to join me later for a light dinner here. She's such a sweet lady."

Grace smiled. "That's a wonderful idea."

Hank fidgeted next to her, his knee bouncing up and down. He was obviously annoyed with the sisters' conversation.

Grace could see that some things hadn't changed over the years with her husband. He was still impatient.

"Everyone asked about you both," Charlotte remarked.

Grace wondered why the others had asked about her and Hank. Were they simply inquiring about why they weren't attending hospitality hour? Or were they asking about their relationship? Grace chided herself for overreacting. But after her trip to town when everyone asked about Hank and wanted to talk about their romantic reunion, she couldn't help but feel like she was living under a microscope.

"Are you sure you don't need my help with anything?" she asked Charlotte.

"No, everything is under control. Go back to enjoying your dinner and conversation." With that, Charlotte left the room.

"Sorry about the interruption," Grace said.

"Is it always like this?" Hank asked.

The door opened again, and Charlotte grimaced. "Sorry," she said as she grabbed a stack of napkins and scooted back out the door.

"We're always on the go when the inn is full," Grace said.

"When do you get time for yourself?" Hank asked, reaching for her hand.

Again, Grace found an excuse to move her hand out of his reach. She assumed he intended to use this dinner as a chance to get reacquainted and rekindle their love. But she wasn't feeling the spark. Maybe she hadn't felt the chemistry between them that they used to have because she'd been putting so much pressure on herself to do so. Perhaps it would return naturally in time.

"Most of the guests leave during the day, so after we've tidied their rooms, we can get away then," she said. "But for the most part, this is what my life is all about."

"Do you enjoy owning an inn?" Hank asked.

Grace nodded. "I love tending to our guests, taking care of my gardens, and meeting new people every week."

"What about your career in marketing?"

"I enjoyed it, but it was time for a change," she said. "I'm thankful for the life I've created here in Magnolia Harbor. It's quiet and slower paced. It may not seem like it at times, but it's an amazing town to live in."

"I get it," he said. "From what I've seen, you're great at what you do here, just like you were at marketing. I didn't mean to push. I've always wanted the best for you."

"There's no need to apologize," Grace said. "It's been a stressful week for both of us."

"You know what the perfect stress buster is? A nice walk along the lake." Hank stood and took her hand.

She hesitated and glanced at the sink of dirty dishes.

"Come on," he urged. "It's a beautiful night. The moon is full, the stars are out, and the cicadas are calling to us."

"Let me leave a note for Charlotte, and I'll grab my sweater."

As if on cue, Winston popped his head out from the hallway leading to her quarters.

"I think someone else wants in on our walk," Hank said. "Does he need to be on a leash?"

"No, Winston is very well-behaved and never takes off. Well, normally. He did earlier, but I think he was chasing a squirrel."

"Let's hope he doesn't take off again tonight." Hank patted his leg. "Come on, boy. Let's go for a walk."

Once they stepped out of the confines and intimacy of the kitchen, Grace could breathe again. Hank was right. It was a perfect night. The moon was full and bright, shining down on Lake Haven. A cool breeze made little ripples across the top of the water. The cicadas sang their song.

The perfect night for a romantic stroll . . . if you were with the one your heart desired.

Perhaps time was all they needed to reconnect. They had been deeply in love when they'd gotten married. It was true they'd been apart for a very long time, but surely their love was still there.

Winston took the lead, glancing over his shoulder to make sure they were following.

Grace and Hank were quiet as they walked.

"Have you thought about what you're going to do for work now that you're back?" Grace asked, breaking the silence.

"I thought I could help run the inn with you," Hank said. "Or maybe I'll search for a job in Charleston."

"What about finding work as an engineer?"

"It's been too long. I'm not current on the most up-to-date technology." Without much enthusiasm, he described what he would need to do to get recertified so he could return to his former field. From there, he launched into more ideas he had for changing her inn. It seemed that he was certain they would work things out.

A few minutes ago, Grace was starting to believe that all they needed to reconnect was time, but now she wasn't so sure. She slipped her sweater over her shoulders and wrapped her arms around her waist to keep Hank from reaching for her hand.

Something was holding her back from getting close to Hank. She wished she knew what it was.

They stopped next to a bench by the water and sat down. Hank slipped one arm around her shoulder.

Grace scooted away. This bench was where she and Spencer often sat. It felt wrong being here with Hank.

Even Winston seemed to feel uncomfortable. The dog sat on the grass between their feet as if trying to keep them apart.

"I've been wanting to give this to you since I arrived." Hank reached into his pocket and removed a small jewelry box. "For the past twenty-two years, this has been in my possession. It's the one link I had to my real life. The one thing that kept me going. The one clue that told me there were two special people waiting for me to come home."

Grace carefully opened the box, unsure and a bit afraid of what she'd find. Inside, on a black velvet cushion, was a necklace with three gold interlocking hearts. She gasped. "It's beautiful."

"I still have the receipt from the jewelry store in Prague where I bought it," he told her. "Do you want to see it?"

Grace blinked back the tears in her eyes. The necklace was such a thoughtful gift and so like the Hank she knew and loved. "No, I don't care about some silly receipt." She closed the box and held it against her heart. "You carried our hearts with you all this time, and you didn't even know it. I'll treasure it always."

Even as the words left her mouth, she still couldn't shake the ugly feeling that something wasn't right.

13

Christie

The Dragonfly Coffee Shop didn't have an empty seat in the house, so Christie hung out at one end of the counter as she waited for Blake to arrive. She didn't mind because it gave her a chance to chat with Angel, the friendly barista.

"I heard that you're a professional investigator or something," Angel said as she poured milk into a stainless steel cup.

"No, I'm a genealogist," Christie said. "While I investigate family trees, I wouldn't call myself a detective or anything."

"That sounds fascinating. You never know what kinds of skeletons you might discover in people's closets." Angel grinned. "Maybe I should have you look into my family tree."

Christie laughed.

When Angel excused herself to wait on another customer, Christie turned to the door. Where was Blake? He'd been begging for this chance to talk, and now he was going to stand her up? That didn't seem likely. She pulled out her phone and checked for messages. Nothing.

As she slipped her phone back into her purse, the bell above the door jingled. She glanced up and saw Blake entering the shop.

He hurried over to her. "Sorry I'm late. Sam called with questions for a new client. It's a big project, so he wanted to make sure he didn't mess up the quote."

"No problem. If I were Sam, I would have called too."

"Did you order yet?" Blake asked.

"No, I was waiting for you," Christie said.

"Are you hungry?" he asked. "Would you like a pastry to go along with your coffee?"

"Sounds good to me."

Christie and Blake put their orders in, then stepped aside to wait.

Blake stood close to her but didn't reach for her as he would have done once. He seemed content to respect her boundaries.

She ignored the small thrill she always felt when Blake was close and turned her attention to the packed coffee shop. Several people were typing on their laptops or cell phones, and a few others were participating in what appeared to be a book club meeting.

Angel called out their names and handed them their coffees and pastries. "Hope you enjoy. Please come back again."

They thanked her and agreed to return.

"We could try to find a bench outside or walk down to the waterfront park," Christie suggested.

"Let's check out the park," Blake said. "It should be quieter at this time of night."

They left the coffee shop and strolled through town. When she shivered at the slight chill in the air, Blake shrugged out of his jacket and draped it around her shoulders. Every now and then she would comment on a store or he would point to something he saw, but for the most part, they walked in companionable silence, enjoying each other's company. Christie was relaxed, and she felt completely at peace with the world.

For those precious minutes, Christie didn't worry about the future. For once, she simply lived for the moment.

"We should do this more often," Blake said quietly.

Christie turned to him and cocked her head. "Do what?"

"Take long walks, spend time alone together." He chuckled and blew out a deep breath. "Yeah, I know that sounds strange coming from me, but maybe I'm learning."

"I didn't say anything."

They arrived at the park, and Blake steered her toward one of the benches with a glorious view of the lake. "You didn't have to say anything. I know I was a horrible boyfriend. But if you give me another chance, I promise I'll do better."

Christie gazed at the moon hanging high and bright, then faced Blake. "First, you weren't a horrible boyfriend. In fact, you were amazing. Like what you did for Grace today." She shrugged and sighed. "That was something straight out of a romance novel."

"Tell me this. Do you still love me?" Hope shined brighter in Blake's eyes than the glow from the full moon.

She didn't want to lead him on, but she couldn't lie. "Very much so."

As her words sunk in, Blake straightened his shoulders. The deep furrows in his forehead and at the corners of his eyes disappeared. His frown shifted, and the edges of his mouth turned upward.

Christie realized that she'd have to be careful about what she said from here on out because she could tell that he thought she'd changed her mind.

Even though Christie longed to reconcile with Blake, the problem hadn't been solved. She hadn't changed her goals. She still wanted marriage and children, and she was still running out of time. "I love you, but it isn't enough."

"It's everything we need."

"You sound like a lovesick teenager," Christie said. "Real relationships don't work that way."

Why had she suggested this coffee date? It appeared that Blake might have changed, but underneath he was still the same sweet guy who believed that only today really mattered. Could she throw her hopes and dreams out the window? Or leave them in the hands of someone who treated them like whims?

"You're overthinking this whole thing," Blake said. "We don't have to plan out every minute of our lives. Haven't we had some great times when we've done things spontaneously?"

"Sure, and that's fine once in a while, but some things in life need to be planned for, like retirement." Christie wanted to bring up the subject of children, but she was afraid that would send him running the other way. Then they'd never finish this conversation, so they'd be doomed to keep having it over and over again. Or he'd offer to marry her for all the wrong reasons—out of pity and obligation instead of love and a desire for a family he wanted as well.

Blake laughed. "We're only in our thirties. We've got a long way to go until we have to think about retiring."

"You say that now, but I'll bet it feels like only yesterday when you were twenty-one," Christie pointed out. "What I'm saying is, life has a way of slipping by. Before you know it, the time you thought was so far off is now upon you, and you don't have any more time to save or prepare for it."

"Okay, I get it," he said, holding up his hands. "You're right. The last ten years have gone by fast, but that's mostly because I've been enjoying life, especially the last three years with you. I want more of that."

At his words, it felt as if her heart were melting and breaking at the same time.

Christie wanted more time with Blake too. She dreamed of spontaneous outings, romantic walks in the moonlight, and moments of laughter over silly things like a dog splashing in a pool. But she also longed to be a mother. She yearned to hold her own child in her arms. Blake had so much patience and love, and she knew he would make an incredible dad. But she couldn't force a life on him that he didn't want.

Her hands trembled, not from the cold but from nerves. She stared into her coffee cup, not making eye contact with him as she tried to find the right words. The last thing she wanted to do was hurt the man she truly loved.

"The past three years have been wonderful," she finally said. "We've had so much fun. Yes, I want more of what we've had, and maybe that's the problem."

"If I'm offering to stick around, how's that a problem?" Blake asked with a frown.

"Because I'm searching for a man to share the rest of my life with," she said. "I need someone who will always be there for me. Someone who will listen to the good and bad that happened during my day and share life's joys and sorrows with me."

"I'm more than willing to do all of that," Blake said.

She gazed into his eyes, and her pulse kicked up a notch when she saw the hope and sincerity there. "As my husband or my boyfriend?"

He shook his head and leaned back against the bench, gazing at the lake. "I told you I'm not ready to get married. Why does it have to be right now?"

And just like that, they were back to square one.

Christie had tried to explain it to him a month ago, and it was as if everything she'd said had been channeled into a box and locked away. He said he heard her, but had he really listened? Since they were right back where they started, she highly doubted it.

For a split second, Christie considered telling him about how her mom and grandmother had gone into early menopause and that there was a good chance it would happen to her. If her doctor was right, Christie's chances of having children of her own were growing bleaker by the month.

But she didn't want Blake to think she was broken or marry her out of pity. She wanted him to choose her because he loved her and wanted all the same things she did.

"I don't even know why we're having this conversation again," Christie said. "You're a great guy. Someday you're going to make some lucky woman a wonderful husband, but it's not going to be me."

"Don't say that," Blake insisted.

She stood. "No, I mean it. I want you to leave me alone and go home. It's over."

Blake sat there, obviously stunned.

Christie whirled around and strode away, swiping at the tears streaming down her face. Saying goodbye to Blake had once again ripped her heart to shreds.

Even though the inn was more than a mile away, she decided to walk. She wouldn't have been able to hold it together if she rode in the same car with Blake for even a short distance.

As she walked, she replayed their conversation. Marriage wasn't completely off the table for Blake. He kept saying it would happen someday. But it was clear that he didn't want to marry her. If she was the one for him, then he wouldn't need to wait. Blake was comfortable in their relationship and didn't want to change it.

By the time Christie arrived at the inn, her tears had dried and it was well past hospitality hour. Hopefully, everyone was either in their rooms or out to dinner because she knew that she looked like a mess. All she wanted to do was sneak up to her room and call her sister. She needed some emotional support.

Christie tried to be quiet by opening the front door slowly, but the bell jingled. As she rushed across the foyer, she heard footsteps. Turning, she saw Charlotte heading toward her.

"Lucinda and I are going to sit down to a light dinner," Charlotte said, then frowned. "What's wrong?"

Before Christie could respond, the tears she'd thought were all dried up burst forth again.

Charlotte wrapped her in a warm hug. "It'll be okay."

Lucinda rounded the corner and joined them. "Come here, child."

Christie stepped out of Charlotte's embrace and went to her other new friend.

Lucinda held Christie tight and rubbed her back as she cried.

"I'll make a pot of tea," Charlotte offered. "Why don't you two relax on the veranda?"

Lucinda nodded, then led Christie to the veranda.

When Christie stopped crying, she found both women sitting with her. Lucinda handed her tissues, and Charlotte gave her a cup of hot tea, then slid a plate of cookies and truffles her way.

"Thank you," Christie said, suddenly realizing she was hungry. She'd skipped dinner and forgotten her pastry at the park with Blake. She grabbed a snickerdoodle. As she nibbled on it, she took the opportunity to collect her thoughts and get her emotions in check.

"If you want to talk, we're here to lend nonjudgmental ears," Charlotte said.

Christie swallowed the lump in her throat and took a sip of hot tea, letting it warm her. She faced Lucinda. "You're going to be so disappointed in me."

"Oh, hogwash," Lucinda said. "I know you had coffee with your young man tonight. That's all I wanted you to do. So how could I be disappointed?"

"We did talk, but nothing has changed," Christie said. "Even though he says he loves me, he doesn't love me enough."

"Maybe he's one of those guys who takes his time when making an important decision," Charlotte suggested. "Perhaps he needs to do research. He might have heard you need to date for a certain amount of years for a marriage to last." She nudged the plate of goodies in Christie's direction.

Christie took one of the chocolate truffles. "We've been dating for three years. And I did an Internet search of that question. Most psychotherapists say it's up to the individuals, but the average is one to two years."

"Did you ask him why he isn't ready?" Lucinda popped one of the truffles into her mouth.

"No, I didn't want him to think I was trying to pressure him into making a decision. I want him to marry me because it's what he wants. Not because it's what he knows I want." Christie set her cup down and inched toward the edge of the chair. "Look, I appreciate your listening ears and support, but I'm interrupting your dinner. You two should go eat and not worry about me. I'll be fine in the morning. I'll take my tea and these snacks up to my room."

"Nonsense. Have you eaten dinner?" Lucinda asked in a don't-argue-with-me tone.

Christie smiled. Her own mother would approve. "No, I haven't."

"I'll set another plate, and you'll join us," Charlotte said. "I made way too much food as usual."

"Thanks," Christie said, thankful for her kind hostess.

"Don't worry," Charlotte said. "Blake will see what he's missing out on, or the right guy will show up and sweep you off your feet when you least expect it."

"I hope it's sooner rather than later," Christie said.

When Charlotte and Lucinda looked at her strangely, she quickly explained her health issues and her heart's longing for children of her own.

Lucinda gave Christie another warm embrace and patted her cheek. "You must follow your heart always. If you're meant to be a mother, then you will be."

Tears welled up in Christie's eyes, and she wiped them away.

"Remember that a child does not have to be born of you to be yours," Lucinda continued. "When the time is right, love will find you, and you will find your heart's desire."

Grace

The next morning, Grace helped Charlotte serve breakfast in the dining room.

Hank and Christie didn't join them, but the rest of the guests had a lively conversation about their plans for the day as they savored their plates of scrambled eggs, English muffins, and bacon.

Grace skipped breakfast. Her stomach was so knotted up that even Charlotte's cooking couldn't tempt her to eat.

When the meal was over, Joel and Felicity took off for the beach, and Monty and Jamie left to help their son pack his dorm room. Lucinda was the only guest remaining as Grace and Charlotte cleaned up.

"I need to get some work done on my cookbook," Charlotte told Grace. "Would you mind if I went to the cottage for a while?"

"Of course not," Grace said. "I'll finish in here."

"Thanks. I'll take these to the kitchen." Charlotte picked up a tray of dirty dishes and left the room.

Lucinda got up. "I think I'll sit on the veranda and enjoy the morning."

"That sounds nice," Grace said. "Can I get you anything else?"

"Maybe another cup of coffee and a blueberry muffin." The older woman laughed. "I certainly haven't lost my appetite during my stay."

"I'll bring them out to you." Grace collected the remaining dishes and carried them to the kitchen. She made a fresh pot of coffee and poured a cup for Lucinda, then put a couple of muffins on a plate.

When Grace stepped onto the veranda, she found Lucinda with Winston on her lap. She smiled. "I see you already have company."

"Indeed," Lucinda said, gently petting the dog. "He's a sweetheart."

"He definitely is." Grace set the cup of coffee and plate of muffins on the table next to her guest.

"Thank you," Lucinda said.

"So, how did you sleep last night?" Grace asked. As a co-owner of the inn, it was more than a polite greeting. Ensuring her guests received a good night's rest was one of her main goals.

"I'd say like a baby," Lucinda said, "but we know they don't sleep well."

Grace chuckled. "That's true, although my son was a pretty good little guy. After the first few months, Jake fell into a regular routine. He would be asleep by eight, then wake up at two and six."

"I don't think I got a good night's sleep for over twenty years with my children," Lucinda said. "If it wasn't feeding time or dirty diapers, it was teething. Then it was potty training and time for the next one to go through the first routine. Once I got them all in school, I thought I'd sleep."

"But that didn't happen?" Grace asked.

Lucinda took a sip of coffee. "No, because once I got the four of them to bed, I needed to get the house picked up or laundry done. Back in those days, I worked outside the home. I swear there were never enough hours in the day to complete my to-do list."

"I still have days like that."

"Me too, and my children are all grown and have families of their own." Lucinda gestured toward one of the empty chairs. "Is your day too busy to enjoy a cup of coffee with an old lady?"

Grace glanced around. "I don't see any old ladies, but I'd love to have coffee with you."

Lucinda chuckled. "I really do like you, Grace Porter. You know how to brighten a person's day."

"I'll be right back," Grace said, then went to the kitchen to pour herself a cup of coffee.

When she returned, Winston was asleep. Grace sat down next to Lucinda.

"You should have one of these muffins," Lucinda said, holding out the plate. "You didn't have breakfast, and I'm betting you haven't eaten anything in hours. You're always too busy taking care of everyone else to think of yourself."

Grace accepted one of the muffins. "Mothering is a hard habit to break. Maybe that's why being an innkeeper works so well for me."

Lucinda nodded before taking a sip of her coffee. "It is a good fit for you and Charlotte."

"Tell me what's on your agenda today," Grace said.

"I was hoping to visit a couple of museums in Charleston," Lucinda replied.

"That sounds nice," Grace said. "Which ones?"

"Patriots Point and the Old Exchange and Provost Dungeon."

"They're excellent choices."

"Patriots Point is for Charley," Lucinda said. "He served on the *USS Yorktown* aircraft carrier."

Grace knew that exploring the ship her husband had once served on would have to bring back many memories for Lucinda. But Grace was sure while many of those would be pleasant, it would also be hard for the lovely woman too.

"It not only received the Presidential Unit Citation, but it earned eleven battle stars for service during World War II," Lucinda went on. "After the war, it was used to recover the *Apollo 8* astronauts and capsule before it was decommissioned in 1970."

Grace smiled. "It sounds like you could be one of the museum's docents."

"Charley and I loved to visit museums when we traveled. We'd find at least one that appealed to both of us. His usually had something to do with the military or farming equipment, and I'd always pick something to do with the history of the area or art."

"It sounds like you had wonderful trips together," Grace remarked.

"We did, but Charley always drove." Lucinda gazed down into her coffee. "To be honest, I'm afraid I'll get lost."

"Why would you think that?" Grace asked. "You drove here and did fine."

"Magnolia Harbor is a small town, and the highway is easy. I get turned around in large cities. There's so much traffic and people honking their horns. Before you know it, the street you were supposed to turn on is right there, and you're not in the correct lane." Lucinda let out a deep sigh, a look of resignation on her face.

Winston, who had been sleeping soundly, lifted his head and gave Lucinda a gentle nudge with his nose.

Lucinda obliged by petting him. "This is why I admire you and Charlotte so much. You're both strong, smart, independent women. Fierce. Not afraid of life."

Grace didn't know about all that. She'd been very afraid of her own emotions lately, and she certainly didn't feel fierce. "From what I've seen, you're exactly the same way. Not many people would go on vacation alone regardless of age or gender. That's a true sign of independence and strength. Plus, you've been a real friend to Christie. Not to mention to me and Charlotte and the rest of the guests. So on top of everything else, you have a gracious heart. Please don't sell yourself short because you don't feel comfortable driving in big cities."

"Thank you for saying so," Lucinda responded. "My children think I'm getting on in years."

"Aren't we all?" Grace laughed gently. "No one's as young as they were the day before."

"Yes, but they think I'm not as sharp as I used to be and that I'm fragile now that Charley's gone," Lucinda said. "I admit that losing him was a blow. I didn't want to leave my house, much less my bed, for days when he first passed."

"But you did," Grace said.

"I did because that rooster wouldn't shut up until I fed the hens." Lucinda laughed. "But I never went to church with my hair in rollers or in my nightgown. I never went shopping and forgot to pay for my groceries."

"What makes your kids think you're having issues?" Grace asked.

"Mentally, I'm fine. They're simply a bunch of mother hens. They want me to sell my place. My oldest said it's too much for me to take care of on my own. I've been doing fine for years. She's only saying that because she thinks I'm going to ask her to come help."

"It sounds like they're worried about you."

"If they were worried, they wouldn't be trying to force me into a retirement home," Lucinda replied. "Sure, they call it 'senior living.' It's one of those fancy setups where you have your own small apartment with a panic button in every room. But they don't even allow the residents to do their own cooking because they're afraid they'll burn the place down."

"It would give you more time for hobbies and fun activities." Grace tried to find the silver lining, but honestly, it didn't sound very uplifting to her either. She couldn't imagine if Jake insisted that she give up the inn someday.

"Like what? Playing bingo? No thanks. That'll keep my mind

going, but I'll gain fifteen pounds the first month from sitting around." Lucinda smacked the table lightly.

The noise caused Winston's head to pop up. Once he realized everything was okay, he settled back down for his nap.

Lucinda took a bite of her muffin. "Then again, if I keep eating Charlotte's cooking, I may gain that much this week alone. But everything she makes is so good."

"She'll be happy to hear you say that," Grace responded. "What do your other children think about you selling?"

"They're all on board. My two middle kids live and work in Nashville, which is a good hour away from the farm. They're worried if something happens they won't be able to get to me in time. I'd say pish-posh, except I did fall last year and broke my arm. I still managed to get myself to the hospital, which I think scared them more than anything."

"And you said you're not fierce and independent," Grace said with a grin. "Of course, you're under no obligation to sell your home or even prove to your family that you're fit, but I get the feeling you'd like to find a way to put their minds at ease."

"What I'd like is for them to stop nagging me and remember I'm their mother," Lucinda said. "I took this trip for two reasons. One was to get a break from my family. I never thought I'd say that. Well, other than when they were teenagers."

Grace laughed. She remembered those days well. Even the best children could drive their mothers to the breaking point, and Jake was no exception. "Have they been worried about you while you're away?"

"Oh my goodness yes. They're calling me constantly. My oldest threatened to have the local police put out a silver alert on me if I didn't tell her where I was going. The youngest put a tracker on my phone. He told me as long as I check in daily he won't tell his sister where I am, and he'll keep her from doing something drastic like filing a missing persons report."

Grace took a sip of her coffee because she wasn't sure what to say. Her own father had passed before her mother, but not once had she ever worried that her mom couldn't take care of herself. Winnie was about Lucinda's age, and she was one of the most active members of Magnolia Harbor. If the family suggested that she and Gus sell their home and move into a senior-living facility, the two would laugh and tell the rest of the family they'd lost their minds.

Not that Grace discounted the need or value in those communities or facilities, but she didn't believe in trying to force a person to give up their independence for someone else's paranoia. From what she'd seen, Lucinda was perfectly capable of continuing to care for herself.

"It sounds like your children love you very much and they're afraid of losing you," Grace said. "I know what it's like to lose a parent and have that fear. I'm not sure if you're aware, but you and I have a few things in common."

"Like what?"

"I was a widow for more than twenty years," Grace answered. "Hank is—was my husband."

Lucinda gave her a confused look.

Grace told her the story of the train crash and how Hank had miraculously reappeared in her life.

"Goodness gracious, child. Now that's some story."

"Yes, it is. As you can see, I do know some of what you're going through with losing a husband."

"Well, let's hope Charley doesn't suddenly reappear because I watched them lower his casket. That would give me a heart attack."

They chuckled. Grace loved how Lucinda managed to laugh when most would cry.

"I've also been in your children's shoes, having lost my father and then found myself constantly worrying about losing my mom," Grace continued. "Not that the worrying stopped it from happening, but it's all part of the process. Grief counseling helped me through the worst of it."

"Thank you for sharing," Lucinda said. "I'm not sure if I can get my children to go to counseling, but I might try that. Maybe if I tell them it's for me, then they'll give it a shot."

"What was the other reason for your trip?" Grace asked. Of course, she thought Magnolia Harbor was the perfect destination, but she was always curious as to what drew outsiders to her small lakeside town.

"I wanted to prove to my children, but mostly to myself, that I wasn't a scared old lady." Lucinda sat up straight and squared her shoulders. "That I could be strong, independent, and smart. That I could take a trip and not get lost. That I could be brave enough to go on my own and meet new people, make new friends, and have new experiences."

Grace smiled.

"If I can't accomplish all that, then they're right, and I'll have to sell my home and move into one of those controlled environments," Lucinda continued. "Then I'll lose all my freedom. I won't get to decide what I want for dinner, and I won't be able to make brownies whenever I crave them. Before I know it, my driver's license will be revoked, and I'll end up being a prisoner shuffled from one activity to the next with no say. That's not the life for me. Not yet anyway. Maybe in another twenty-five years when I'm actually old, but even then I'd like to think I'll be a handful for the staff."

"I don't see that happening anytime soon," Grace said. "But when the time comes, I'm sure you'll keep things interesting for the staff and in ways they'll look forward to."

Winston woke up and yipped as if in agreement.

The women laughed.

Lucinda reached into her purse and pulled out a couple of sheets of paper. "I printed out these directions on how to get to Patriots Point and the Old Exchange. Can you check and make sure it's the best route from here? While I might be smart enough to look up directions, I'm also savvy enough to know to double-check with a local before I start my adventure."

Grace studied the route map and gave Lucinda a few shortcuts to avoid the congested areas of Charleston. "You'll have a wonderful time exploring today. Be sure to take some photos to show your family when you get home."

"Thank you," Lucinda said as she stuffed the papers into her purse. After gently setting Winston on the chair cushion, she stood. She gazed at the lawn and then down again as if struggling with what she wanted to say.

Grace remained silent as she drank her coffee, waiting for her guest to speak.

Lucinda sat back down. "There is something else I was hoping to ask your advice about since you've been in my situation before. Granted, it's a little different as your son was so young when you were first widowed, but how did you handle dating?"

Grace recalled a previous conversation when Lucinda had mentioned that a man had asked her to dinner but she'd turned him down. "Are you referring to Buck?"

Lucinda rolled and unrolled her napkin on the table, avoiding eye contact with Grace. "Yes. He goes to my church and lives next door. I've known him for years."

Grace smiled. "That's good."

"He used to play cards with Charley and help him with harvesting and the animals when it was more than one person could handle," Lucinda said. "Buck has asked me out for dinner a couple of times now."

"Do you want to have dinner with him?" Grace asked.

Lucinda looked at her with a shimmer of tears in her eyes. "I do, but I feel like I'm cheating on Charley with his best friend. Then there's the children's reaction. I'm not sure I'm up to dealing with more of their drama, but I'm not ready to disappear from life."

Grace reached out and took both of Lucinda's hands in hers and held tight. Oh, how she remembered the doubts and fears of her first date after Hank's death. She'd experienced so much guilt. She'd worried she was adding to Jake's trauma and what her family and friends would think. She'd wondered if it was too soon, if he would measure up to Hank, and if anyone could ever love her like Hank had.

"There are no set rules or guidelines to being a widow," Grace said. "There's no timeline on how long we're supposed to grieve or when we should jump into the social world of dating. It's different for each of us."

"When will I know when the time is right?" Lucinda asked.

"Give it some time and patience and listen to your heart."

Lucinda smiled. "That's good advice. I'd encourage you to follow it too."

Grace

After Lucinda left, Grace grabbed her basket and garden shears and headed out to clip fresh flowers for the rooms. Winston joined her.

Hank and Christie had still not come downstairs, but she'd left a basket of muffins, a bowl of fresh fruit, and a pot of coffee for them in the dining room.

There was too much to do for her to sit around waiting for them. Charlotte was on a conference call with her editor, so all the work landed on her. Not that Grace minded. She enjoyed the busy work, the simple tasks of straightening up the suites and gathering flowers in the garden.

As she worked, she couldn't help but think about her failed dinner date with Hank. Life would almost be easier if he had shown up and said that he'd had amnesia and married someone else while he'd been away. It would have made perfect sense. Actually, she realized it was a little odd that he hadn't found someone else and fallen in love. Hank was a good-looking man, and he must have dated over the years. So why hadn't he found love since he'd been gone?

But Grace was the last person to throw stones or question why. She had dated occasionally after Hank's supposed passing, but she hadn't formed any serious relationships. Until recently, she hadn't found anyone she truly connected with. Of course in her case, she had been grieving the loss of her husband while taking care of a young son, trying to balance a job and create the semblance of a normal home. For the longest time, she'd had neither the time nor the energy to date.

She could only imagine what those early days had been like for Hank. Surely he'd been lost, confused, lonely, and even a bit scared.

Hank had said that though he couldn't remember anything about his life, he knew he had someone out there waiting for him. The necklace was proof. Maybe that was what had kept him from making any lasting commitments over the years.

After he'd held out so long to find her, what if they weren't meant to be together? What if Hank had met someone in Europe and dismissed her, his real true love, because of Grace, a woman he couldn't remember? Would Hank be alone forever because of her if they didn't reconcile?

And what about Spencer?

The urge to scream and throw herself on the bed made Grace laugh as she snipped some fresh baby's breath. She hadn't been this torn up over someone since high school. Except this time around the stakes were much higher.

She filled her basket with flowers and turned to Winston. "Are you ready to go inside?"

Charlotte stepped out of her cottage and trotted over. "I'm glad I caught you. Can you spare a few minutes to talk?"

Grace studied her sister's anxious expression. "Of course."

"Let's go to my cottage," Charlotte said, leading the way.

Winston followed them inside. The dog retreated to a bed Charlotte kept for him.

Grace sat on the couch. She'd always liked the cottage with its wood beams and Charlotte's eclectic taste. Grace motioned to the geometric runner on the kitchen table. It was a gift from a former guest, and Grace had received an identical runner. "Eden's gotten quite good at quilting since she was here."

"She definitely has," Charlotte said as she dropped into the chair. She twisted her hands together and bit down on her lower lip.

Tension rolled off her sister in waves, and Grace worried that Charlotte's newest cookbook contract had been canceled. "You had a call with your editor and publishing team this morning," Grace said softly. "Did everything go okay? You seem a bit stressed."

"Yes, I did," Charlotte said. "Sales are still steady for my last book, so that was good news. The marketing concept for the new book isn't exactly what I envisioned, but it was only a draft. I'm sure the final will be much better."

"If you need any help, please don't hesitate to ask. It's been a few years, but I don't think I've forgotten everything about marketing." Grace knew this wasn't what her sister wanted to talk about, but she could tell Charlotte needed a moment to gather her thoughts and decide how to tackle the subject.

"Thanks. I appreciate it," Charlotte said. "I also called my attorney because I had a few contract questions for her. While I had her on the phone, I asked her about the situation with Hank since your attorney is on vacation. I hope you don't feel I overstepped, but since the inn is involved, I felt I had a right."

Grace had been so caught up in her own emotional struggles that she'd failed to fully understand how Hank's reappearance affected her sister. It hadn't occurred to her that Charlotte might be feeling unsure of her place in Grace's life and the business now too. "Of course not. I'll be glad to finally get some answers. It's hard not knowing."

"Whew." Charlotte blew out a breath and laughed. "I'm so relieved."

"I want to apologize for not asking you how you're feeling," Grace said. "Hank's return affects all of us, not just Jake and me."

"It's all right," Charlotte said. "I know you're on an emotional roller coaster. I can't imagine what you're going through. It's a situation that no one could have ever imagined."

"Why don't you pour us something to drink?" Grace suggested. "I'll forward the landline to my cell phone, so we can talk here in private."

"Sounds good. I'll make a pot of tea and get a snack." Charlotte went to the adjoining kitchen and put a kettle on the stove.

Grace watched her sister awkwardly move around the kitchen. Charlotte dropped a chocolate chip cookie on the floor when she was putting them on a plate, and she slammed the door of the cupboard after retrieving two cups. Clearly, Charlotte's conversation with her attorney had upset her. The kitchen was Charlotte's sanctuary, a place where she didn't allow negative energy, so her clumsy actions meant something was really bothering her.

After the water had boiled, Charlotte poured the tea and put the cups and plate of cookies on a tray. She carried the tray to the living room and set it on the coffee table.

The two of them settled into their seats again, and Grace kept her phone next to her in case they received any calls at the inn.

"What did you and your attorney talk about?" Grace asked, then blew gently on her tea.

"I explained the situation of Hank's death and his reappearance," Charlotte replied.

"And?" Grace set the cup down and leaned forward.

"After she got over her shock, I asked her if you and Hank were still legally married."

"Are we?" Grace asked, clasping her hands together to stop them from trembling. She was a jumble of nerves. At the moment, she honestly didn't know which answer she wanted to hear.

Charlotte reached over, took one of Grace's hands, and gently squeezed it. "No, you're not. Once he was declared dead, you were released from the union."

"But he's not dead," Grace said. "Doesn't that void the declaration?"

"No, apparently it fulfills the 'until death do us part' thing. It's over, but we don't say 'until death do us part, however many times that happens.' It's kind of weird. You were a widow, but now you're not. However, you're still single."

Grace huffed out a laugh and blinked back tears. "I don't even know which box to check on paperwork now." She wiped the corners of her eyes. As she allowed the news to sink in, she tried to gauge how she was feeling. Finally, she decided that she was too numb to feel much of anything.

"Are you okay?" Charlotte asked, studying her.

"I realize it sounds strange, but I am okay," Grace answered. "Now that I know the answer to that question, I feel a sense of peace, and I don't feel quite as lost as I did. Thank you."

Grace also felt like she had regained some control of her life. If she and Hank found their lost connection, they could always remarry. And if not, they could go their separate ways.

"I'm glad to hear that," Charlotte said.

"But I am curious about why you talked to your attorney today," Grace said. "You knew I had an appointment set up with my attorney next week."

Charlotte nibbled on a cookie. "Have you and Hank talked about your relationship yet? I'm sure my barging in and out of dinner last night didn't help."

Grace blinked at the apparent subject change but decided to follow her sister's lead. "You were only doing what needed to be done—taking care of our guests. As for Hank and me, not really. Last night was more about getting to know him again." She tilted her head. "Why are you asking?"

"I'll be honest. He rubs me the wrong way. I spoke to my attorney because the thought of being in business with this new Hank Porter turns my stomach, and I needed to know if he had a claim to the inn like he said."

Grace shot straight up, her feet hitting the floor with a thud. "He said what?"

Winston jumped out of the bed and raced to her side. He glanced from one sister to the other, whining in distress until Grace stroked his back to calm him.

"I'm sorry. That's not how I meant to tell you," Charlotte said. "He made me so mad yesterday while you were out running errands."

"What did he do?" Grace asked.

"While I was cleaning one of the rooms, he stopped by. No, it was more like he strolled in as if he owned it. Then he ran his finger across the top of the dresser and inspected it with a huff. He glanced around and declared the room was too provincial."

"He told me that we should modernize, but I shot down his suggestion." Grace got up and paced across the small living room as she considered how to handle her former spouse.

"It's not the only suggestion he made," Charlotte admitted.

Grace stopped and stared at her. "What else did he say?"

"He asked what was on the menu for hospitality hour," Charlotte said. "After I rattled off the appetizers, he had the nerve to tell me that next time I should check with him first."

"Why in the world would you talk to him about it?" Grace asked, stunned.

"He reminded me that he's spent years in high-end hotels in Europe and he could make the inn more sophisticated."

Grace returned to the couch and put her head in her hands.

Winston reached up and set his little front paws on her legs.

Grace smiled and rubbed his ears to show she was okay, but the dog knew better. He didn't leave her side. "I'm so sorry. I had no idea."

"I set him straight and told him I run the kitchen," Charlotte said. "If he didn't like what I was serving, he was welcome to skip our hospitality hour and enjoy whatever was on the menu at the restaurant of his choice."

"The kitchen is—as it always has been and always will be—your domain," Grace said firmly.

"But then he made several other comments," Charlotte said. "And a few times last night when I walked into the kitchen, he had such a smug look on his face that I thought maybe the two of you were getting back together."

Grace gave her sister a big hug. When she let go, she saw tears in Charlotte's eyes. "First, thank you for asking. Second, regardless of what happens between Hank and me, the inn is yours and mine. I may be the older sister, but we're equals in the business."

"I don't think Hank sees it that way," Charlotte said. "The last time he saw me, I was a teenager, and he's still probably trying to reconcile that image with the person I am now. It's probably overwhelming to him."

"We're trying to reconcile that he's not a ghost," Grace said, then realized her comment had sounded harsh. "I mean, this is an adjustment period for all of us. If Hank is having trouble getting used to a grown-up Charlotte, imagine what will happen when he meets a grown-up Jake."

"Good point," Charlotte said.

"Don't worry," Grace said. "If Hank and I were to renew our vows—and honestly, that's a big if right now—then I would make sure the inn was protected, just in case. I won't think about only myself in this."

"I take it last night didn't go as well as you'd hoped."

"No, I wouldn't say that. More that it didn't go as Hank had hoped. I wanted to get to know Hank better, see the man he's become after all these years. I think I caught a glimpse. But something tells me that he was hoping for more, and that simply didn't happen. It's too soon, and there's so much going on."

"Are you referring to Spencer?" Charlotte asked.

Grace nodded. "I care deeply for Spencer. He's a dear friend, and above everything else, I don't want to see him get hurt. It was so simple before. All those emotions surrounding Hank had been locked away in a part of my heart, and I moved on."

"Until he showed up on our doorstep as alive as you and me," Charlotte added.

"Exactly. At first, I thought it would be the same for Hank, that he'd tell me he'd moved on and that he was simply here to let me know he's alive and to reconnect with Jake. Then he springs this whole story on me about how he always knew there was someone waiting for him, but he couldn't remember me. He's held on to a necklace for twenty-two years, waiting to find me and give it to me."

"Wow," Charlotte said. "Now I feel bad for disliking him."

"It's okay. After what he said to you, it's understandable." Grace bit her lip, then decided to come clean with her sister. "I did get a peek at the new Hank, and I'm not sure we mesh. He's very different than the man I married. He's polished and chic, and while he's been living in Europe, he's also become very modern and urban. I like my quiet life in the country."

"Are you afraid he'll get bored?" Charlotte asked.

"I think he already is," Grace said. "For instance, what does he do all day?"

"Besides tell me how to do my job?" Charlotte asked with an arched brow. "Maybe he hangs out in Magnolia Harbor."

"I'm not sure," Grace said. "From my trip into town yesterday, it didn't sound like a lot of people have actually seen Hank. However, everyone knows what happened."

"If they're not hearing it from Hank, then how did they find out?"

Grace chuckled. "You know this town. One word said in the right place can travel for miles. Captain Daley stopped me, so there's a good chance Dolly might have heard him talking."

Dolly Batten, the dispatcher at the police department, loved to talk. She had a tendency to let things slip, and everyone knew to watch what they said to Dolly, even though she would never spread lies or secrets to intentionally hurt someone.

"That makes sense," Charlotte said. "So, if Hank's not hanging out in town, where does he go every day?"

"He mentioned that he might search for a job in Charleston, but he hasn't told me if he's gone there yet."

"You should ask him. If he expects to share your life again, you deserve to know what his looks like now. What does he have to hide?"

Charlotte had a point. Grace should ask a lot more questions. If they were going to make a go of things again, she needed to know Hank's plans for the future, and she needed to make it clear that the inn was hers and Charlotte's business alone.

Perhaps Hank planned to return to Europe. While she would love to visit Austria, her home would always be in South Carolina. Walking down cobblestone streets and exploring castles would be a dream come true, but she couldn't imagine giving up her Spanish moss, lovely magnolia trees, and the wonderful people of Magnolia Harbor.

Of course, after last night and the total lack of chemistry, Grace wasn't sure she even thought they had a future together other than being former spouses and Jake's parents. Hopefully, they would always be friends.

Maybe this coming weekend, after all the guests left and before the next wave arrived, she and Hank could sit down and have a long talk. They needed to go somewhere they wouldn't be interrupted. If nothing else, they needed to share and be honest with each other about how they were feeling and what their hopes were for their relationship. The courts said they were no longer married, but in her heart, she couldn't ignore the vows and promises they'd made on their wedding day.

On the other hand, when they'd promised for better or worse more than twenty-five years before, they never could have predicted they'd find themselves in this bizarre situation.

As she silently struggled with the moral dilemma, her phone pinged with an incoming message. It was from Spencer.

> *Sorry I haven't been over. I'm helping a friend with a problem, but you've been on my mind. Let me know if you need anything. Miss you.*

It was a sweet gesture, but it reminded her of one more dilemma she needed to solve.

16

Grace

While the sisters hired the local lawn care company Two Green Thumbs to maintain the grounds of the inn, Grace still took every chance she could to work in the flower beds.

After her conversation with Charlotte, Grace tended to her plants. She reveled in the way the sun warmed her back and the breeze kissed her cheeks. In fact, she almost forgot she was working. Leaving the corporate world behind to open the inn with her sister had been the best decision she'd ever made, although not an easy one. In the beginning, there had been many sleepless nights filled with worry.

She hadn't been that stressed until now. While there had been lean and tough times, she had been confident in her choice and knew she and Charlotte could make the inn successful. She had faith in them and in herself. But this week everything was different. Maybe it was harder because it wasn't a business decision. Instead, it was a choice that involved her heart.

Yet Charlotte's parting words after their chat kept ringing in her ears. "Maybe you don't feel the same way about Hank because you've already given your heart away to another."

Grace wouldn't go so far as to say she'd boxed up her heart in a pretty little package, complete with a bow, and handed it to Spencer. But it might be edging closer in that direction. Maybe she'd get there if it weren't for the giant pothole in front of her demanding her attention and the detour sign pointing in the opposite direction.

Grace never wanted to rush into anything. She liked to take her time, consider the pros and cons, weigh her options, and let everything happen organically when she had the opportunity. But at the moment, it was like being at a stop sign, with a line of cars behind her honking to hurry up.

She snipped a dead flower and then another and another before sighing and dropping her hand. At this rate, it would look like a herd of deer had binged on her poor dahlias. She should go beat the area rugs instead, except no one did that in this day and age. If they did, it would help work out their frustrations. As would churning butter or scrubbing laundry by hand. Maybe it would benefit her and Charlotte if they started offering demonstrations on what life used to be like in the South. She smiled at the notion.

Winston came running around the side of the house and dropped to his haunches before rolling over onto his back.

Grace sat down next to him and rubbed his belly. Her dog had the right idea. Instead of beating rugs or churning butter, she needed to relax and focus on what she had control over. Stressing over every little thing never helped anyone.

As she and Winston enjoyed the gorgeous May afternoon playing a game of fetch with a tennis ball, a car pulled up. Grace caught a glimpse of Christie and waved. She stood and dusted off her knees before tossing the ball again.

Christie got out of her car and walked over to Grace.

"Did you have a nice day?" Grace asked.

Christie nodded. "Now that I'm done with my genealogy project, the rest of my time here is strictly a vacation. So I had a massage and went shopping for my mom's birthday."

"Did you find her a present?" Grace asked.

Winston brought his ball over and dropped it at Christie's feet.

Christie scratched the dog's ears and chucked him under the chin before tossing the ball. "I stumbled onto a great antique store and bought a few collector's plates and an old wall phone, the kind with a crank from the early 1900s. She's going to love them."

"What great finds. I'd love to have one of those phones, but I don't know where I'd put it." Grace pulled off her work gloves and tossed them into the basket. "It sounds like a relaxing way to spend your day."

Christie dropped down onto the grass to play tug-of-war with Winston and his ball. "I asked Lucinda to join me, but she was determined to visit those museums in Charleston today. When I offered to go with her, she told me no thanks. She said she had to go alone."

"You two seem to have gotten very close," Grace remarked. "I think it's been good for her."

"It's been good for me as well. Lucinda has become like a grandmother to me," Christie said. "Do you know if she's back?"

"Not yet but I'm not surprised," Grace answered. "Those museums can take hours to explore. I wouldn't expect her until hospitality hour. Have you tried calling or texting to check on her?"

"Oh no, I don't want to sound like her kids and make her think I have no faith in her," Christie replied. "That's not why I was asking. I thought she'd get a kick out of seeing what I bought at the antique store." She frowned. "Besides, I have some phone calls to make."

"Is everything all right?" Grace asked, noticing the frustration in her guest's tone. She hoped it wasn't another fight between Christie and Blake. They were both wonderful, and Grace was pulling for the two of them to work things out. But she didn't want to pry into their personal lives.

"My credit card company sent me a possible fraud notification," Christie explained. "It was a large online purchase from a store in New York. I denied the charge, and the company froze the account."

"That's good," Grace said. "It sounds like you've taken care of it."

"Not entirely. There was another charge from a jewelry store in Charleston the other day that I didn't make. Now I need to check on my other cards and call my bank."

"How terrible," Grace said. "But I'm sure your credit card company won't hold you responsible for the charges."

"I don't think they will. I'm more worried about something else."

"What is it? Are you concerned that they hacked your other accounts?" Grace had a friend who had been a victim of identity theft, and it had been awful. It had taken her months to deal with all the claims.

"There's that, but if my accounts are all frozen, how am I going to pay for my bill here at the inn?" Christie's cheeks flamed red as tears glistened at the corners of her eyes.

"Let's not worry about that at the moment," Grace said. "You're not planning to leave today, are you?"

"No."

"Call the bank and your other cards to find out if they've been hacked, and let them know what's going on. You need to protect yourself first. If they have to freeze everything, I understand. We can always work out a payment plan for your stay if necessary."

"But I have the money in the bank," Christie said. "It's in my special travel fund. I'm afraid I won't be able to access it or that whoever gained access to my credit card might have drained it. Honestly, I didn't make that purchase. Why would I buy diamond cuff links? I don't wear them, and I don't know anyone who would. My dad would shake his head and laugh at me."

"Is that what the thief bought?" Grace asked.

"That was one of the items, along with a necklace," Christie said.

"Did they steal your actual credit card?"

"No, I still have the card, so I didn't notice at first," Christie said. "Since I'm staying near Charleston, it looked like I made the purchase."

"That's awful," Grace said. "I'm so sorry you're dealing with this."

"I have to call the fraud department," Christie said. "But I don't even know if I should call the police in Charleston, Magnolia Harbor, or my hometown."

"I'm sure the fraud department can help you," Grace assured her. "If not, I can call my neighbor Spencer Lewis. He's retired from the FBI, but he might know someone who can help. And I'm sure the police captain in town could be of assistance."

"Thanks. Let me see what the credit card company says. If they give me the runaround, I'll take you up on your offer."

"Sounds good."

"As long as my bank hasn't frozen everything," Christie continued, "I'll ask my mom to get a cashier's check for the bill and overnight the check. Otherwise, it'll take up to ten days for the replacement card to arrive."

"I appreciate your letting me know," Grace said. "If your mom can't run to the bank, be sure to tell Charlotte or me, and we'll work it out. I have complete faith in you."

Christie threw herself into Grace's arms and gave her a tight hug. "Thank you. Surprisingly, this has been the best vacation ever. I'm really going to miss you and Charlotte and Lucinda when I go home."

"We're going to miss you too," Grace said. "We hope you'll visit us again sometime."

"I'm planning on it." Christie stepped away and swiped at her eyes with the back of her hand. "I'd better go and make those calls. Thanks for understanding."

After Christie was gone, Grace thought about their conversation. Christie had said it was the best vacation ever, but it seemed to Grace that her guest's trip had been a bit cursed. First, it appeared as if someone had snooped through Christie's room, and now there were fraudulent charges on her credit card. Had someone broken into Christie's room and stolen her credit card number?

Winston barked, jolting Grace out of her reverie.

Grace glanced down and saw his ball resting on the grass at her feet. She picked it up and tossed it.

Winston chased the ball and returned it to her.

"I think that's enough for today," Grace said with a laugh. "Let's go inside."

Winston wagged his tail.

Grace went to her quarters with Winston on her heels.

She retrieved her laptop and searched for information on basic security systems. It seemed like a good time to look into installing a system. Not only did they have their guests and belongings to think about but also some priceless antiques at the inn and a few expensive personal items. Thinking of her personal items reminded her that she needed to update her insurance list and add the necklace Hank gave her.

The one still sitting in its box on her dresser that she couldn't bring herself to wear.

Grace

Friday morning, Grace stood in the kitchen gazing out at the lake.

The inn was empty. Charlotte was at her cottage, Lucinda was taking a trip to the coast, Christie was shopping, the Bensons were spending the day in Charleston, and the Robinsons were at their son's graduation events. Grace had no idea where Hank had gone. He hadn't joined them for breakfast, and at first she'd thought he was sleeping in, but his rental car wasn't parked out front.

Now was the perfect time to clean the suites. If only she could tear herself away from the view. It was another gorgeous day with the sun glistening off the water and blue skies with white fluffy clouds floating overhead. But that wasn't what held her attention. No, it was the lone egret standing at the edge of the lake.

She couldn't even say that she was deep in thought about the events unfolding in her life. The only thing going through her mind was the bird, with its solitary and simple existence. Envy for the egret swept over her, and for one moment she wished she could spread her wings and fly away, leaving all the chaos of her emotions behind.

But of course that wouldn't solve anything. The problem would still be waiting for her when she returned. Grace laughed and shook her head as she stepped away from the window. *Blame it on the lack of sleep.*

During the previous night's hospitality hour, Christie had told her that a cashier's check was being overnighted to the inn and that so far none of her other accounts had been touched. To be safe, she'd requested that all her cards be reissued with new numbers on them.

She had also set an alert on her bank accounts. While Grace had been relieved to hear that her guest hadn't had her savings drained, she still felt responsible. She feared that someone had broken into Christie's room and accessed her credit card.

Grace was thankful that the situation hadn't been any worse, but if it had originated at the inn, then it was a problem. She needed to safeguard the well-being and safety of her guests.

At this point, Grace wasn't even sure someone had broken into the inn. It was possible Christie's card had been scanned at a gas station or even while out shopping or dining. However, the inn had been a victim of theft before, and she was taking this incident as another warning.

She'd left a message with a representative of the security system, but she wanted to talk to Spencer and get his thoughts too. As a retired FBI agent, he would know more about what they needed. If they decided to purchase a system, she had no idea how extensive it would need to be to protect their inn without intruding on their guests' privacy.

Grace figured the rooms could wait a few more minutes while she called Spencer.

As she headed to her private quarters to grab her cell phone, she couldn't ignore the small thrill racing through her at the mere thought of hearing his voice. Between his trip to Washington and the busy week, she'd missed him. She'd missed his easy smile that lit up his eyes. The way he made her laugh and how simply being with him felt right. She missed their conversations and the easy friendship between them. When he looked at her, she experienced excitement, not of love blooming—not yet—but of knowing that what they had could become something more.

Suddenly, Winston bounded over to the back door. The dog whined and danced around.

Grace peeked out the window and grinned. "It seems I'm not the only one who missed my friend, but we mustn't appear overly eager."

The dog spun in a circle on his hind legs and barked.

Grace laughed and opened the back door.

Spencer stood there, appearing stunned. "Let me guess," he said with a smile. "Winston gave us away?"

She nodded.

"Bailey was so anxious to get here," he said. "She ran in circles around me, urging me to walk faster. She really missed her friend."

I did too. Grace bent down to scratch Bailey behind the ears, then stepped aside for Winston to race out the door, down the stairs, and across the lawn with the Lab right behind him.

They watched the two dogs for a moment.

Spencer gave her a warm hug. "I hope you don't mind us stopping by unannounced." He handed her a small bag. "Charlotte asked if I could drop off some pecans."

"Of course not," Grace assured him. "I've never minded before, so why would I now? Nothing's changed, and you don't need an excuse like dropping off pecans either."

"I'm glad," he said.

"Would you like to come inside and have some coffee?" Grace asked.

"I won't turn down a cup," Spencer said, his eyes twinkling.

Grace led the way into the kitchen. She set the bag of pecans on the counter, then went to the coffeepot and poured two cups.

He took the cup she held out. "I know you've got your hands full right now, and I didn't want to add to your stress, but I've been worried about you."

"Thank you. I appreciate that more than you know."

"Anytime," he said, and the warmth in his tone melted some of her worry.

She motioned to the back door. "Let's go outside so we can watch the dogs."

They took their cups of coffee outside and sat on the steps. The dogs were playing tag and soaking up the morning sun.

"How are you holding up with a full house?" Spencer asked. "And having Hank around again?"

"Honestly, the full house is keeping me going and giving me a sense of normalcy." Grace wasn't sure what to say about Hank. She didn't know how she felt about her once-dead-now-alive husband. And when she tried to picture her future, all she could see was an outline of a man, but she couldn't tell if it was Hank or Spencer.

But she could barely admit these feelings to herself, much less share them with the man she'd gone on a few dates with. She hadn't even shared them with Charlotte or Winnie.

"Is he pressuring you for money?" Spencer asked, furrowing his brows. "Or anything else?"

"No, he's mostly given me space." It wasn't totally true, but Grace could sense Spencer's concern, and for now, she needed to figure this out on her own. "We've been slowly getting reacquainted. He's changed a lot. But it has been a long time. I've changed too." She swirled the coffee around in her cup. "I think he's nervous about meeting Jake more than anything."

"Does Hank know that we've gone out?" he asked.

Grace met his inquiring stare. "I'm not sure. I haven't hidden the fact, but I also haven't told him. While we've talked, it's been more about him and what he's gone through all these years."

"Don't you think he should know?" Spencer asked.

"Yes, he should," she said. "I guess I haven't told him because I haven't really opened up and talked much about my life. It's still hard to think of him as my former husband."

"But he is, and it doesn't sound like he thinks of himself as your *former* anything. He definitely doesn't consider himself another guest at the inn."

"How do you know that?"

"Charlotte. When she asked me to bring over the pecans, she mentioned a comment he'd made."

Grace drew in a deep breath and let it out slowly.

"Please don't get mad at her," he said. "She was frustrated and needed someone to vent to. I happened to be handy."

"I'm not mad at her. She and I talked about it yesterday. I had no idea Hank was making suggestions to her about changing things around here. I was going to talk to him about boundaries this morning, but he didn't show for breakfast and his car's not here."

Spencer dropped his gaze. "I don't want you to get mad at me either, but I think you should know I have a friend looking into Hank's story. I know he's the man you married and Jake's father, but he's been gone a long time. I don't want you to get hurt."

She blinked at him in surprise, then smiled. How very like Spencer to go the extra mile to protect someone he cared about. "Thank you. I appreciate your concern. But I was hoping to get your help with another matter."

"What's going on?" he asked.

Grace filled Spencer in on the issue with Christie's credit card, her safety concerns, and the idea of installing a security system.

Spencer agreed the security system was a good idea and took Grace on a tour of the inn, pointing out potential camera locations and weak areas where someone could easily gain access to the inside.

She wrote everything down, along with the type of system he suggested.

Afterward, they ended up in the kitchen.

"I didn't realize how vulnerable we were, but I feel better knowing what to look for and how to protect our guests," Grace said. "Let me see how Charlotte feels about installing the system before I make any final decisions."

"If she has any questions, tell her to give me a call," Spencer said. "Is there anything else I can do to help?"

"Not unless you want to clean the guest rooms," she joked.

"Which ones?" he asked. "Just point me in the right direction."

"I was kidding, but I do appreciate the offer. Charlotte should be back soon, and we'll get them done quickly."

"I'm surprised Winnie isn't over here," Spencer commented.

"She's been notably absent this week. Maybe she needs a break," Grace said. "To be honest, I'm looking forward to having a few hours to myself with nothing pressing to do."

"I can give you a break and take you to lunch," he said, hopefulness filling his voice.

"That sounds wonderful," Grace said. "I wish I could say yes, but as soon as I get done here I have to dash into town to talk to Pastor Abrams about the fundraiser."

"How about a rain check?"

"It's Charlotte's turn to watch the inn on Sunday," Grace said, "so we could have brunch at The Tidewater after church."

Grace and Charlotte alternated weekends to attend church so one of them could take care of the inn.

"Sounds like a plan," Spencer said.

The bell above the front door jingled.

"I'd better go and let you get to work," he said. "Tell Charlotte if she has any leftover pecans, she's welcome to make a pie for me."

"You and your sweet tooth." Grace laughed as she waved Spencer off and called Winston into the house.

The dog flopped down on the floor, obviously exhausted.

The door to the kitchen opened, and her sister breezed in with a bag of groceries. "Sorry it took me so long, but I stopped at Hanson's and talked to Cal for a while."

Cal Gunderson was the friendly owner of Hanson's Farm Fresh Foods. It was one of their favorite local markets.

"Check out these peaches," Charlotte said, removing a container from the bag. "I'm thinking pie or muffins."

"Speaking of pies, Spencer dropped off the pecans you asked for."

"That explains your improved mood," Charlotte teased. She removed the rest of the groceries from the bag and started putting them away.

"I don't know what you're talking about," Grace muttered. "Why did you want pecans if you're going to make a peach pie?"

"Oh, those will be for the church fundraiser," Charlotte replied. "I promised to donate a couple of pies and a basket."

"I'm sure Penny will appreciate it," Grace said.

Putting the pastor's wife, Penny Abrams, in charge of the fundraiser had been a brilliant idea. No one ever said no to her.

"Penny also asked if we'd be willing to donate a sweetheart package from the inn," Charlotte said. "It would include dinner on the veranda and a night in one of the suites complete with champagne and chocolate-covered strawberries, then breakfast the next morning. What do you think?"

"It's a great idea, but it could get awkward to have two people dining when we've told the rest of the guests we don't serve dinner."

"Maybe I could get Dean to donate dinner at The Tidewater and the rest would be from us."

"Sounds perfect," Grace said. "After I clean the guest rooms, I'm attending a meeting about the fundraiser, so I'll let Penny know about the sweetheart package."

"I'll lend you a hand with the rooms," Charlotte offered.

Between the two of them, they tidied up the suites in no time. Winston got his second wind and followed them from room to room.

Charlotte insisted on taking care of the other chores so Grace could slip out and complete her errands.

"Thanks," Grace said, grabbing her purse. She patted Winston on the head and told him to be a good boy, then drove to downtown Magnolia Harbor.

Her first stop was the fundraiser meeting at the Fellowship Christian Church. Grace gave the others an update on the tasks she'd been assigned and confirmed with Penny that the inn would donate a sweetheart package.

After the meeting, Grace went to the bank and popped into her attorney's office. Even though he was out on vacation, Grace wanted to leave a brief message about her upcoming appointment. She had concerns about the insurance company and their payout. Would they demand the money back and with interest? Could the inn be in any jeopardy? She had to make sure their livelihood was protected.

As Grace was walking to her car, she spotted Winnie across the street. Grace smiled and waved at her aunt before running across the street to join her. "I feel like I haven't seen you in ages. Is everything all right at home? Gus isn't sick, is he?"

Her aunt linked her arm through Grace's and started walking. "Goodness no, dear. He's fine."

Grace studied Winnie's neutral expression and started to worry. Her aunt didn't do neutral. "I'm glad to hear that. It's unusual for you not to stop by on your morning walks, so . . ." She let her sentence trail off, hoping Winnie would share more.

"Let's get some coffee at the Dragonfly and talk," Winnie suggested.

Grace's insides churned. She hadn't heard that tone in Winnie's voice in a long time, and she wasn't sure she wanted to hear what came next.

Grace and Winnie walked to the Dragonfly and went to the counter.

"Oh, those cupcakes look delicious," Grace said.

"You should get them for the inn," Winnie said. "I'm sure Charlotte won't mind, and cake is always a great way to celebrate."

"What are we celebrating?" Grace asked.

"I don't know, but you've got an inn full of guests."

"Who are all leaving tomorrow," Grace reminded her. "If they don't eat the cupcakes, they'll go to waste." She grinned. "Or rather, my waistline."

With a sigh from her aunt, they each ordered a coffee and a pastry instead.

"You two take a seat, and I'll bring your order over in a moment. These are so much better warm," Angel said as she popped the cheese-and-fruit strudels into the oven.

"Let's sit at the table in the corner," Winnie said. "It's a little quieter there."

Grace's stomach continued to churn. It reminded her of when she was in high school and Winnie had found out about her skipping a class. Her aunt had never told her parents, but she'd given Grace a long lecture on honesty that day.

Once they were seated, Grace said, "Okay, tell me what's wrong."

"Nothing's wrong." Winnie patted her arm. "How are you doing? I'm sure it hasn't been an easy week for you. You never have liked chaos."

"I'm fine," Grace answered. "A little tired but that's to be expected with a full inn."

"And Hank? How are you two getting along?" Winnie sighed. "I imagine now that he's in the picture you'll be making a lot of changes."

A thought hit Grace, and she cringed. "Have you been staying away from the inn because of Hank? Did he say something to you to make you feel unwelcome?"

"Well, no, not really," her aunt replied. "He told me that I don't need to pop in and check on you so much because he'll be helping out now. He said it would give me a chance to enjoy my golden years."

"What?" Grace asked, appalled. She reined in her anger when Angel brought over their food and drinks. After thanking her friend, she turned to her aunt. "First, I'm sorry I haven't checked in with you before today, and I'm doubly sorry if Hank made you feel unwanted or unneeded at the inn."

"There's no need to apologize," Winnie said. "You've had your hands full."

"I do, but that's no excuse," Grace said. "Charlotte and I love you, and we truly enjoy your frequent visits. So do our guests. We can't thank you enough for pitching in. You're a crucial part of the inn. If you need a break, that's fine, but if you want to come over, please don't hesitate."

"I know you girls don't mind," her aunt said. "But things are changing."

"No, they're not," Grace insisted. "At least, not at the inn. It's business as usual. So please ignore what Hank said and know that I'll be having a word with him."

Winnie frowned. "I didn't mean to stir up trouble."

"You didn't stir up trouble," Grace said. "Hank did. To be honest, he's been overstepping since he arrived." She paused. "He's definitely not the same man I married."

"After more than two decades, no one would be." Winnie blew on her hot coffee and watched her, probably to see if Grace picked up on her meaning.

"I know it would be silly to expect that the events of that awful day and everything that's happened to him since then wouldn't change him," Grace said. "But it seems like he's a totally different person. If I wasn't so sure it was really him, I'd buy into Spencer's theory that the man calling himself Hank Porter is a scam artist."

"So, what are you going to do?" Winnie asked.

"I don't know, but I'll figure it out."

"Well, I know what I'm going to do," Winnie declared, a mischievous glint in her eyes.

"And what's that?" Grace asked with a smile.

"I'm going to buy those cupcakes, just in case."

Christie

Christie was worried about Lucinda. She hadn't seen her new friend since the day before.

Christie left her suite and walked downstairs, searching for the older woman. When Christie stepped onto the back veranda, she saw Charlotte sitting in one of the chairs and typing on her laptop.

Charlotte glanced up and blinked a few times as if she were trying to clear her mind.

"I'm sorry for interrupting," Christie said. "You're in the middle of something."

"No worries," Charlotte said. "I was editing a recipe description. I can't seem to get it quite right. Can I help you with something?"

"Have you seen Lucinda today?" Christie asked, taking a seat. "I made dinner reservations at The Tidewater for tonight and was hoping she would join me since we'll both be leaving tomorrow."

"I haven't seen her since this morning," Charlotte replied. "She popped in when I was making breakfast and said she was going sightseeing along the coast today. I gave her a cup of coffee to go along with a couple of muffins and some fruit, but I didn't ask when she'd be back."

Christie smiled. "Good for her. It sounds like her trip to Charleston got her over her fear of venturing out on her own. Did she say how her day at the museums went?"

"No, but she seemed to be in good spirits." Charlotte closed her laptop and sat back. "I'm assuming that means everything went well."

Before Christie could respond, Winston dashed out onto the veranda, sat at her feet, and barked.

Christie laughed.

The dog spun around in a circle and barked, then ran inside the house. A moment later, he raced back to the doorway, cocked his head, and barked again.

"I think Winston wants you to follow him," Charlotte said.

"What does he want?" Christie asked.

Charlotte shrugged.

Christie and Charlotte got up and followed the dog into the house. Grace met them in the foyer.

"What's up with Winston?" Christie asked.

"He wanted to tell you that you have a visitor," Grace said.

Peeking out the window, Christie spotted Blake getting out of his truck. "For Pete's sake. This has got to stop."

Christie stormed out the door, then came to an abrupt halt on the front steps. Thoughts of sending him packing temporarily fled her mind as she gaped at Blake. He was dressed to the nines, and he held a huge bouquet of red roses. Even though the temperature was in the eighties, he wore a black suit with a red button-down shirt, sans the tie, and shiny new black shoes. He had to be melting in this heat and humidity, but it was all for nothing. She was done listening.

Blake took a step toward her and smiled. His expression was so full of hope and happiness and love that Christie melted a little herself.

"Stop, please." Christie held up her hand before he could come any closer. The last thing her resolve needed was to find out if he smelled as good as he looked. After all the effort he'd put into this, it would be hard enough to turn him down. "Save whatever you're planning to say. I'm done, we're over, and you need to move on. You need to let me move on."

"We're not over," Blake said. "We've barely begun."

Christie laughed but refused to be baited into the same old argument. They'd begun three years ago. Compared to Lucinda's love story, they'd barely started, but she refused to be a forever girlfriend with no promise of a future together.

She wanted that promise. She needed the reassurance that she was worth the commitment, but Blake didn't understand the value of a piece of paper. He believed that simply saying he loved her was enough. Christie cherished hearing those three little words, but she wanted the action to prove he meant them. Maybe that was wrong. It probably was. She should be happy that he loved her. It should be enough, but it wasn't. She wanted more.

"I know you think you love me, but you don't," Christie said. "At least, not like I love you, because if you did you'd be able to commit to me for a lifetime. And you can't or won't. Either way, I need someone who loves me enough to make that commitment. I need someone who isn't afraid to promise me forever. I deserve someone who loves me as much as I love them."

"You're wrong," Blake said. "You don't know what you're talking about."

"Excuse me?" Christie narrowed her eyes and put both hands on her hips, fuming. Of all the things he could have said, it was the last thing she'd expected or needed to hear. Not if he wanted back in her good graces. "It doesn't matter anymore. We're done. Go away."

"Give me five minutes," Blake said. "If you still feel the same way, then I'll get in my truck and drive away. You'll never see or hear from me again."

Christie remained silent, wondering what to say.

He gave her the lopsided, goofy smile that had worked a hundred times before. "Isn't it worth knowing if you're throwing away forever or not?"

She frowned. He was being unfair. After all this time, after countless talks and too many tears to count, he dangled her dream in front of her. "I'm listening." She glanced at her watch. "And counting."

"Fair enough," Blake said with a chuckle. Then he turned serious. "First, I do love you. I love you more than anything in this world. More than I ever thought was possible to love someone. I go to sleep with you on my mind every night. I wake up every morning thinking of you and seeing your beautiful smile, wanting to hear your laugh. I can't imagine my life without you."

Tears that sprang from hope and love and sorrow filled her eyes. She wiped them away, then focused on the man before her. "Those are pretty words, but I've heard them before."

"I'm not finished. When you brought up taking the next step—getting married—I wasn't ready, but it didn't mean that I would never be ready."

"What are you saying?" she asked cautiously.

"I can't imagine not being married to you," Blake said. "But I wanted to do it right. I didn't want you to have any regrets."

Her heart sped up at the words. Words given freely and said with love. "Wait a minute. Why would I have any regrets? Do you think I would have stayed with you for the past three years if I didn't know without a doubt that I love you? I've known since our first date that you're the man I wanted to spend my life with."

"I've known since the moment I saw you," he said.

Christie descended the steps. "Then why would you think I'd regret marrying you?"

"I know you want a home, a family, the whole package, just like your sister has," Blake said. "I didn't want to propose until I could give you everything."

"What do you mean?" she asked.

"I've been working extra hours and taking on more projects so I could make my business a success, one that would support us and save for the down payment on the house you showed me. If I can offer you the home of your dreams, you'd know I meant forever when I asked you to marry me."

"Blake." She took a step toward him. How could she have been so foolish and unaware? Yes, she'd shown him a picture of her dream home, but that was just it... a dream. She had never considered actually buying a house that expensive.

"The business is doing great, and it looks like it'll only get better," Blake continued. "I don't have the down payment for the house yet, but if you give me another chance, I'll find a second job and come up with the money."

Closing her eyes, she fought back a tidal wave of tears.

He reached into his pocket, then dropped to one knee and held out a small black velvet box. "Promise me forever, Christie. Will you marry me?"

Christie gasped and covered her mouth with her hands. Suddenly, she decided that it didn't matter if he wanted children. The two of them being together was all that counted.

She took the last few steps to Blake and accepted the box. She didn't open it right away, not that she wasn't dying to see the contents. But first she needed to set a few things straight.

"Come on. Stand up." She couldn't help but laugh at the giddiness flooding through her. "You should have talked to me and had a little more faith in me. Yes, I loved that house as a dream, not reality. I mean, it was half a million dollars. I don't need a big home, just one filled with love. Besides, I've been saving too. Between the two of us, maybe we can find a place we both like. I don't care if it's small as long as you're with me."

"Is that a yes?" Blake asked, hope shining in his eyes.

Tears trickled down her cheeks, and a grin she couldn't suppress spread wide. "Say it again."

"Christie Ann Thompson, I love you, and if you marry me, I'll spend every day of the rest of our lives proving it to you. Please say yes."

She nodded, unable to get the words past the lump of emotions in her throat. Then she threw herself into Blake's arms, laughing and crying the happiest of tears. "Yes," she whispered. "Yes, a million times over."

Clapping and cheers broke out all around them.

Wiping her cheeks dry, Christie turned to see Lucinda standing next to her car, crying and smiling. Grace and Charlotte and the rest of the guests stood on the front steps with Winston, who danced in place.

Blake cupped her face and kissed her tenderly. "You didn't even look at the ring."

"Because it doesn't matter," Christie said. "It could be made out of string, and I still would have said yes."

Taking the box from her shaking hands, Blake opened it.

She sucked in her breath. It definitely wasn't made of string. A sparkling round diamond sat at the center with twin sets of amethyst stones on each side that resembled pale-purple leaves. "It's beautiful. Thank you."

Blake smiled. "It's not as beautiful as you, but I'm glad you like it."

After he slipped the ring onto her finger, her new friends surrounded them, wishing the two of them many joyful years together.

"We wish you all the happiness we've had over the years," Monty said. He hugged Christie and clapped Blake on the shoulder.

"What a story to tell your children someday," Jamie remarked. "If you have a daughter, you should name her Magnolia in honor of this place."

"Magnolia?" Monty laughed. "The poor kid will be teased horribly at school."

"They can call her Maggie for short," Jamie replied.

"It's a little early to think of baby names," Christie said. "I mean, we should probably tell our families and set a date first."

"I think Magnolia is the perfect name for our daughter." Blake grinned and pulled Christie close to his side.

Her heart soared at his response.

"Congratulations," Hank said, holding out his hand to Blake. "I hope there are no hard feelings about when I tried to chase you off."

Blake hesitated before shaking the man's hand. "None taken. You were just watching out for Christie. I appreciate it."

Joel stepped forward next. "Want a tip from a recent groom? Just agree with anything she suggests for the wedding. You'll be a happier man if you do."

Felicity playfully slapped his arm. "Hey, you told me to do whatever I wanted." She leaned toward Christie and whispered, "If you need any tips, feel free to contact me."

"Oh, I sense a good story there," Christie said with a laugh. "I'll be sure to give you my number so you can tell me about it."

"You might want to consider eloping," Felicity suggested. "Then you won't end up with your fourth cousin twice removed who drives you crazy as a bridesmaid."

"I'm afraid that won't be an option," Christie said. "My mother would never forgive us."

Felicity turned to Blake and grinned. "If you win over her mom, then you're golden. Don't even try with her dad. He may have liked you before, but the minute he hears you're taking his daughter away, all bets are off."

They laughed.

Grace and Charlotte hugged them next.

"I'm so glad you didn't give up," Grace said to Blake. "I knew from the start that you two were made for each other. This definitely calls for a celebration."

"I'll get the champagne," Charlotte said.

"And we have cupcakes courtesy of Winnie," Grace added. She glanced at her sister, and the two of them chuckled.

"What's so funny?" Joel asked.

"It was Winnie's idea to buy the cupcakes," Grace answered. "Leave it to her to know exactly what we needed."

As everyone turned to go inside, Winston jumped up, planted his front paws on Blake's leg, and barked.

"What's up, boy?" Blake asked.

"I believe he's congratulating you," Grace said.

Blake scooped up the little dog and rubbed his ears. "I think he's trying to tell us the first addition we make to our family should be a dog of our own."

"Is that so, Winston?" Christie asked.

Winston gave a sharp bark in return, causing the group to laugh.

As the others headed inside, Christie hung back to talk with Lucinda. She was anxious to catch up with her. "How was your trip into Charleston yesterday?"

"It was good." Lucinda hugged Christie and kissed her on the cheek. "We'll talk about it later. Right now it's all about you and your young man."

"Please tell me you'll come to the wedding," Christie said. "If you hadn't made me promise to keep my heart open, we wouldn't have anything to celebrate."

"There's nothing in this world that could stop me from being there," Lucinda said.

Christie smiled, her heart full of love and happiness. She was thankful for the past few days and the friends she'd made, as well as the future that lay ahead of her with the man of her dreams.

19

Grace

On Saturday morning, Blake joined Christie and the rest of the guests for a special celebratory breakfast.

Charlotte pulled out all the stops. She made orange dream mimosas to toast the new couple, creamy garlic-herb quiches, and cheese crostini with pecans and bacon. To top it off, she prepared spiced peach puffs and mixed berry tartlets. No one was walking away hungry this morning, and Grace was sure each and every guest would leave the Magnolia Harbor Inn with fond memories of their stay and the delicious food.

Grace didn't think she'd seen a happier setting, but her focus wasn't entirely on the newly engaged couple. She was still struggling with her own dilemma.

Charlotte entered the dining room, her hands full of dishes. "This is the last of it. You should sit and enjoy."

"Only if you will," Grace said.

"You both need to join us," Christie said. "We insist."

Grace and Charlotte took seats at each end of the table and started passing plates of food around.

"I never had a chance to ask how your trip to Charleston went the other day," Grace said to Lucinda.

The older woman set a spiced peach puff on her plate, then sat back and laughed. "It was quite an adventure."

"Did you meet someone tall, dark, and handsome?" Christie winked as she handed Lucinda the berry tartlets.

"Oh, listen to this one," Lucinda teased. "She's preoccupied with love now."

The group laughed and joked, but Grace caught the momentary flash of sadness in Lucinda's eyes. Had something bad happened on her outing?

"Well, as a matter of fact, I did meet someone," Lucinda said. "Thankfully, he was a policeman and very helpful."

"What happened?" Christie asked, concern in her tone.

"I got lost as usual," Lucinda answered. "Charley used to claim I could get lost going from one room to another in our own home. He wasn't wrong on some days."

The others protested.

"It's all right. I ended up where I wanted to go," Lucinda said, waving off their comments. "But it did make me wonder if my children are right. Maybe I am too old to be on my own."

"That's nonsense," Christie said. "I've spent a great deal of time with you, and you're as sharp as a tack. Don't let them bully you into a retirement home."

"I'm not letting them do that," Lucinda said. "When I was about to give up and return to the inn, I remembered the compass Winnie gave me. And I used it to guide me to my destination and back here."

"How wonderful," Grace said.

"Leave it to Winnie," Charlotte said. "She always knows what people need before they even need it."

"Your kind words before I left helped too," Lucinda told Grace. "You reminded me that I'm more resilient than my children give me credit for." She glanced at Hank. "You also reminded me that just because I lost my Charley, it doesn't mean my life is over."

Grace was relieved when Lucinda didn't say anything else on that matter. "I'm glad my words were of comfort and gave you strength when you needed them."

"They did, but I have to admit my children aren't completely wrong," Lucinda said. "I am getting older, and taking care of the farm is a lot of work."

"Are you going to put it up for sale?" Monty asked.

His wife put her hand on his arm and shook her head.

"It's okay," Lucinda assured Jamie. "The answer is no, at least not yet. I do need help around the old place, so I'm going to hire the two teenagers who live down the road from me to do the heavier chores. They're good boys, and they've been asking me to let them help out lately."

"That sounds like a perfect compromise." Grace hoped Lucinda's children would be satisfied with the idea and realize how important it was for their mother to remain independent.

"I also realized something else," Lucinda said, excitement sparking her blue eyes. "An adventure is good for the soul. Routines are fine as long as we don't allow ourselves to fall into a rut. That's what causes us to age faster. I'm going to shake things up a little more when I get home."

"What are you planning to do?" Charlotte asked.

"I'm going to say yes to Buck, a nice man from my church who's been asking me out for months," Lucinda said. "After all, a cup of coffee and a slice of pie between friends can't hurt."

Unbeknownst to Grace, her aunt had arrived while Lucinda was talking to the group. It wasn't until Winnie started clapping that anyone noticed her standing in the doorway.

"Bravo," Winnie said. "Take it from another seasoned lady. You're never too old for some sweetness in your life."

The group pulled up another chair and made room for Winnie to join the party. Food was passed around, and plates were refilled.

Charlotte topped off glasses, and more toasts were made. Those who had been married for a long time shared stories for not only the recently engaged but the newlyweds.

Every now and then, Grace would catch Hank watching her. As much as she had wanted to join the celebration that morning, she also wanted to keep her distance from Hank. They had things to discuss. Or rather, she had things to tell him.

Long after the plates and glasses were emptied, the guests finally started to excuse themselves to pack, and Winnie returned home to check on Gus.

It had been a good week, and Grace would miss each and every guest, especially Lucinda, Christie, and Blake, even though he technically wasn't a guest. She stopped at the kitchen sink and watched the lone egret at the water's edge.

"What are you looking at?" Charlotte asked.

"An egret." Grace turned to her. "It seems to like that section of the lake. I think we need to name our long-legged friend since it's becoming a permanent fixture."

Charlotte gazed out the window. "What should we call him?"

"*Sola*, which is Spanish for 'alone.' I think it's a female."

"You think she's lonesome?"

"I do, or at least that's how I feel when I see her standing out there all alone."

Charlotte wrapped her arms around Grace and hugged her tight. "Are you okay? You seem sad this morning."

"It's always bittersweet when special guests leave," Grace said. "But it's more than that. I've made a decision about other areas in my life, and I need to deal with that as well. It's made me a little melancholy."

"Let me know if you want to talk about it," Charlotte said.

"Thank you. I will." Grace excused herself to go find Hank. Putting off the inevitable wouldn't make it any easier, and quite frankly, she didn't even know if he planned to check out today or not.

Winston accompanied Grace as she searched for Hank. As she rounded the corner into the foyer, Hank walked down the stairs, tossing his car keys.

"It's a beautiful day," Hank said. "Care to go for a ride with me?"

"No thank you. I have chores to take care of here at the inn. However, I do need a couple of minutes of your time. Can we step into the other room and talk?"

"Sure. Lead the way." Hank, obviously in a playful mood, bowed and held out his hand.

Grace ignored the gesture and walked into the formal living room with Winston trailing. She took a seat on one of the sofas, and Winston hopped onto her lap.

Hank sat next to her.

She cuddled the dog on her lap, suddenly very nervous. What she was doing was the right thing, but that didn't mean she relished the task. "I'm not sure where to start." She had hoped to keep her tone calm and level, maybe even a bit upbeat to show this was a good thing, but tears clogged the back of her throat.

"Just say what's on your mind," Hank told her. "What's this about?"

"Us." Grace took a deep breath and gazed at the man she'd once promised to love for the rest of her life. "After the shock of seeing you wore off, I was hoping that I'd rediscover the spark that used to be between us and fall back in love with you."

"But you didn't." It wasn't a question.

"No, I didn't. So much time has passed since you disappeared. Too much time. We're not the same people anymore." Grace sighed. "I'm sorry, but I don't love you."

"Even if I had made it home all those years ago, we still wouldn't be the same people today that we were then," Hank argued. "People change. They grow up."

"But we would have done it together," she said. "Your years in Europe changed your tastes, interests, and goals. Your heart isn't here in a small town in South Carolina, and mine is."

Quitting had never been her style, and Grace hated giving up on them, especially when she felt like she hadn't even really given them a chance. But she needed to listen to her instincts, and they screamed that she and this version of Hank were not meant to be together.

"Is this because of that guy you've been dating?" Hank asked, his tone edged with anger.

Grace wondered how Hank had found out about Spencer, but she didn't want to dwell on that now. "No, it has nothing to do with him." She leaned forward to catch his eye. "What you and I had was special. Magical even."

"It can be again," he said.

"I'll never regret our time together because you made me very happy and we had Jake," Grace said. "The chemistry between us is different now. It's tense where it used to be easy, and we no longer laugh all the time like we used to."

Hank reached for her hand and squeezed it. "Give me a chance, and I'll make you laugh."

"It's too late. I think we're trying to be those crazy kids in love when we both know we're not and never will be. We need to admit it's over." Tears welled at the corners of her eyes, and she reminded herself that this was the right thing to do. This new Hank didn't fit into her world, she'd never fit into his, and neither of them deserved to be trapped in a loveless marriage.

"You're absolutely sure this is what you want?" Hank asked, avoiding her gaze. "It hasn't even been a week."

"I'm positive."

He let go of her hand and stood. "What's next?"

"I have an appointment with my attorney next week," Grace said. "From what I've learned, our marriage was dissolved when you were declared dead, and your resurfacing doesn't change that. However, I'll double-check with him. If I need to, I'll ask him to start any necessary paperwork to officially end it."

He smirked. "You're not worried I'll fight you on a divorce?"

"No, because you know I'm right, and I'm pretty sure we're already free of each other and our commitment."

"That's true," Hank said. "You've been through enough, and I'd never drag you into a legal battle. So, what about Jake?"

"You're still his father, of course," she said. "He'll be here Tuesday, so you can see him then. Or you're welcome to make arrangements to meet up with him in Raleigh."

"Do you mind if I stay here tonight while I make plans with Jake?" he asked.

Before she could answer, she heard the bell over the front door jingle and Charlotte greet their arrivals. Spencer's voice didn't surprise Grace, but hearing Captain Daley startled her. It was unusual for him to stop by the inn unannounced. Grace strained to hear the conversation, but all she could make out were snippets—first her name and then Hank's. What was going on?

Charlotte knocked on the door and poked her head into the room. "Would you both join us in the foyer?"

"It had better not be another dead relative showing up," Grace muttered.

Grace and Winston followed Hank into the foyer, where Spencer, Captain Daley, and Officers Wesley Townsend and Greg Warshaw waited for them. The sight of the stern policemen in uniform sent chills throughout her body. She prayed that nothing had happened to Jake.

The Bensons and Robinsons were halfway down the stairs, and Lucinda, Christie, and Blake were at the top. They were all frozen in place as they watched the scene below.

Grace put on her best professional face and smiled at the captain. "How can we help you?"

"I'm sorry to do this," Captain Daley told her, then approached Hank, his officers following suit. "Hank Porter, you're under arrest."

The whole room gasped, and Winston whined.

Grace stumbled, and as she reached out for something to hold on to, strong hands gripped her elbows and held her up. *Spencer.* She closed her eyes, fighting the tears.

"What are you talking about?" Hank sputtered. "What are the charges?"

"We'll start with entering the United States on a false ID," Daley said. "Then there are the multiple European countries that would like to talk to you about credit card fraud and theft." He raised his brows. "It seems you had a nice little operation going at several upscale restaurants and hotels, cloning credit card numbers and room keys."

"All lies," Hank protested. "I was only a waiter. They should be searching for my former roommate. He stiffed me for the last month's rent and cleaned out my savings account. I had to hock everything I owned to get back to the States."

"From what I understand, they found your roommate and partner, and he told them everything," the captain said. "We've also been tracing your movements since you arrived here a month ago."

"What?" Grace blurted out, then faced Hank. "You said you came straight to the inn to see me. What else did you lie about? Are you even Hank or just some man who resembles him?"

"Unfortunately, he's Hank," Spencer said. "We've tested his DNA and confirmed it."

Hank smirked. "My DNA was never on file anywhere, so where did you get a sample?"

"Jake," Spencer said simply.

"Cuff him, read him his rights, and get him out of here," Captain Daley instructed Officer Townsend.

"Wait." Grace broke free from Spencer's hold and strode over to the captain. "You said you've been tracking Hank's movements since he arrived in the States. What does that mean?"

"Maybe we should discuss this later," Daley suggested, glancing at the guests still standing on the stairs.

"No, I want to know now." It was more than that. Grace had to know. Who was Hank Porter?

"Since he arrived in the States, we've discovered a series of hotel robberies everywhere he went," Daley explained. "The robberies match the ones he's wanted for in Europe. We also uncovered reports of credit card fraud in the same locations."

Hotel robberies. Credit card fraud. The words swirled around in Grace's mind. How could she have been so blind? Christie had thought someone had been in her room, but Grace had never imagined it could have been another guest. And not just any guest but her own husband.

The father of her child was an international criminal.

A week ago, her life had made sense. Everything was moving along nicely. Her son was doing fabulous at work. Her family was well. Business was booming, and her friendship with Spencer was deepening. Then she'd opened the door to a ghost and a thief.

Grace stared Hank in the eye. "Did you break into Christie's room and steal her credit card information? Save the lies. I want the whole truth."

"What's one more charge?" Hank sneered. "Yeah, that was me."

"Why would you do something like that?" Grace asked.

"I needed something to soften you up, but I was low on funds," Hank said. "I bought you the necklace and then a pair of cuff links that I sold to get the cash. The part about my roommate cleaning me out was the truth."

"You told me you purchased the necklace at a jewelry store in Prague twenty-two years ago. It reminded you that you had a family waiting for you somewhere," Grace said quietly. "And you claimed to have the receipt."

"I do have a receipt," Hank said. "But it's fake."

"And everything else you've told me since you got here?" Grace persisted. "Was any of that true?"

"I knew I had someone special waiting for me here," Hank answered. "But the rest was just a story. I wasn't even on the train that day."

"How can you say that?" Grace asked, crossing her arms over her chest. "You have a scar from the accident."

Hank snorted. "It was a car accident."

Grace struggled to make sense of what Hank was saying. "Why weren't you on the train?"

"I was late to the station," Hank said. "As I stood there and watched the train pull away, it felt like a sign. My life was miserable, and nothing was going as I had planned."

Grace's heart broke into a million pieces as Hank's words sank in. He had chosen not to come home to her, to let her believe he was dead.

"When I heard about the train crash, it was like a second sign," Hank continued. "There was my chance to start again. I could begin a new life. No bills weighing me down. No responsibilities of marriage or fatherhood. No one to let down. Or I could come home and face all my coworkers, knowing two of my colleagues had died and I should have too."

"So you took the easy way out?" Grace asked. It didn't matter what he said because she'd stopped feeling. Everything was numb. From her head to her toes, there was nothing. She couldn't even feel her heart beating anymore. The only indication that she was still alive was the shallow rise and fall of her chest. So she focused on simply breathing.

Hank reached out to her, but she jerked her arm away.

"I was young and scared and overwhelmed between work and home," Hank told her. "I made a mistake, but I came back. I really did want a second chance with you and Jake."

"By lying to us and stealing from my guests?" Grace stared into his green eyes, eyes she'd once known intimately. But now they belonged to a complete stranger. "Don't bother answering. It'll just be another lie." She turned to the captain. "Please get this man out of here."

20

Grace

As the police escorted Hank away, Charlotte walked up to Grace and slipped her arm around her waist.

Flanked by people who cared about her, Grace watched the man who had sworn to love her through good times and bad, the father of her child, truly die. Their support gave her the strength to hold her head high and carry on when all she wanted to do was curl up in bed and cry. How could she have been so blind?

"Why don't you go into your quarters and rest?" Charlotte asked.

"Not now. We have guests to take care of." Grace gently freed herself from Charlotte's embrace and faced Spencer. "We'll talk as soon as Charlotte and I have checked out the guests. Is that all right?"

He nodded.

Grace took his hand and squeezed it, then stepped around the desk.

Never one to stand around and be idle, Spencer offered to take the luggage out to the waiting cars.

The Robinsons and Bensons approached the desk, their eyes wary and full of concern. Who could blame them? They'd been staying with an international felon for the past week. The reviews alone could tank the inn's business.

"I can't even begin to apologize for what you just witnessed," Grace said. "Please be assured that Charlotte and I had no idea of Mr. Porter's European activities. If you find any of your personal belongings have gone missing from your rooms, please let us know, and we will reimburse you."

Jamie rested her hand on Grace's arm and smiled. It was soft, sad, and filled with kindness that almost brought Grace to her knees. "Nothing went missing from our room, and there were no signs that anyone other than you or Charlotte had been in there to clean. We had the most amazing time at your lovely inn. As for what just happened, there's no reason for you to apologize. He made those decisions, not you."

Monty shook Grace's hand. "I agree with my wife. We had a great stay, and we'll definitely be back."

"Thank you for making our honeymoon so memorable," Felicity said. "The inn is beautiful. But all the little touches you added to our room—such as the fresh flowers and the chocolates, having the fireplace ready to go, and sending up breakfast—made it perfect. We loved every minute of it."

"We certainly did," Joel said. "Maybe we'll return next year on our anniversary." He glanced at his bride for her reaction.

"I think that would be wonderful," Felicity said. "Can we reserve the same room now?"

The happiness and the hope in her guests' comments warmed Grace's heart. Hank's treachery hadn't ruined their vacations after all. "I'll make a note of it, and then we'll send you a confirmation in six months to make sure nothing has changed. Thank you all for staying with us."

"Also, as a thank-you, we're giving you a complimentary copy of my latest cookbook, if you'd like one." Charlotte held out a copy to each couple, and they eagerly accepted the books before leaving.

As soon as they were alone, Grace turned to Charlotte. "Given the situation, I feel we should comp Christie's stay and refund her payment. A member of our family stole from her."

"I agree," Charlotte said. "It's the right thing to do."

Spencer walked inside and joined them. "How are you ladies doing?"

"I'm in shock," Grace admitted. "I can't wrap my head around the fact that Hank went from being a well-respected engineer to a thief. How does that even happen?"

"Setting up a new life in another country while hiding under a false identity isn't as easy as Hank assumed it would be," Spencer said. "First of all, he couldn't use his degree to land an engineering job. Obtaining a fake ID is fairly cheap, but getting other papers, such as false transcripts and birth certificates, is very expensive. As you said, he took the easy way out."

Before they could continue the conversation, the rest of the guests made their way down the stairs.

"We want to thank you for staying with us," Charlotte said. "Please accept my latest cookbook." She handed copies to Christie and Lucinda.

The women were delighted.

Grace plastered on a smile and faced Lucinda. "It has been such a pleasure having you stay with us. I hope this morning hasn't ruined your vacation."

"Oh, nonsense." Lucinda leaned in closer and whispered, "I never did take a liking to Hank, and I believe you're much better off with this one." She smiled at Spencer.

Grace ducked her head as her cheeks heated. "Please stay in touch and let me know how things go with Buck."

"I will," Lucinda promised. "Maybe he'll be my plus-one, and you'll get to meet him then."

"What do you mean?" Grace asked.

Christie laughed and Blake grinned.

"Lucinda spoiled our surprise," Christie said. "If it's all right, we'd like to get married here. It seems fitting."

Winston danced around the couple, obviously excited about the news.

Charlotte squealed and threw her arms around Christie and Blake. "We'd love to host the wedding. And we know a wonderful wedding planner who will do a marvelous job."

Grace hugged the couple. "If you give me a minute to check out Lucinda, we can peek at the calendar and even block out a few dates for the ceremony."

Christie and Blake agreed.

Once Grace had everything settled for Lucinda, Spencer offered to carry her suitcase to her car.

"We want to apologize to you for this morning," Grace said to Christie. "And especially for Hank's actions. We can't change what happened, but we can try to make up for it a little. Your stay is on us. It's the least we can do."

"No, there's no need. I want to—"

Charlotte held up her hand, cutting off Christie's argument. "It's pointless arguing with my sister when she sets her mind to something."

They laughed.

"We're really sorry about what happened," Charlotte continued. "But we're thrilled you're going to have your wedding here. Now let's talk dates."

Grace retrieved the calendar, and they marked a couple of potential weekends so the couple could confirm with their family first. Charlotte promised she'd have Rochelle Earnhart, the county's most popular wedding planner, get in touch with them soon.

"Thank you so much," Christie said. "We appreciate it."

Blake picked up Christie's suitcase. "Are you ready?"

Christie nodded, and the two of them left the inn holding hands.

Once all the guests were gone, Grace no longer needed to remain strong and professional. The energy and strength she had summoned earlier suddenly vanished.

Charlotte put her arm around Grace's shoulders. "Since no one is checking in until tomorrow, why don't you take the rest of the day off? I'll take care of anything that comes up."

"Thank you," Grace said. But she knew she couldn't rest yet. Spencer was still outside, and they needed to talk. "When Spencer comes in, would you let him know that I'm in my quarters and send him that way for me?"

"Sure," Charlotte said. "Are you all right?"

"Yes, just really tired."

"That's understandable," Charlotte said. "This week has been one big shock after another."

"I don't know which shock was bigger—Hank being alive or his nefarious new career. He wasn't the man I married, and I'm not sure if he ever was who I thought, since he was able to walk away so easily."

Charlotte took her sister's hand for a moment. "I know. It's a lot to deal with. But you don't have to do it alone. You have me and Winnie, among others. We're right here, and we're exactly who you think we are."

"Thank you," Grace said. It took everything she had to walk the short distance to her private quarters. Winston joined her. She collapsed into her chair and wrapped herself in a soft blanket.

Winston hopped onto her lap and licked her chin, then curled up into a ball and went to sleep.

Grace cuddled the sweet dog. Winston was such a comforting presence in her life.

She didn't know how long she sat there with her hand resting on her dog's back before Spencer showed up.

The light knock on her door brought her out of her emotional fog.

"Come in," she called.

When Spencer opened the door, she met his concerned gaze. She stirred to an upright position and shook off the blanket.

Winston jumped down and greeted Spencer, then trotted to his dog bed. Instead of going to sleep, he watched them, evidently waiting until he was needed again.

"I'm sorry about what happened." Spencer sat on the ottoman in front of her and took her cold hands in his strong, warm ones. "We didn't want to arrest Hank in front of your other guests, but given his track record, we also didn't want to give him the chance to bolt."

"No need to apologize. I understand, and I appreciate you watching out for me and Charlotte and discovering the truth." Grace raised her eyebrows. "Was I the friend you referenced in your text the other day? The one you said needed help?"

He nodded. "I was working with Quinton to dig into Hank's past. The information we needed to confirm our suspicions and make the arrest came through this morning. Quinton will be arriving in a little while to take Hank into FBI custody."

"I still can't believe he's the same man I married," Grace said.

"It's a lot to process."

Grace sighed. It was all too much. "What am I going to tell Jake? He's going to be devastated. He lost his father at such a young age, he gets him back, and before he can even meet him, he's going to lose him to the prison system."

"Jake will be okay," Spencer assured her. "He's strong and smart, and he has you. He doesn't know the full story as to why we needed his DNA, but he knows that Hank was a person of interest in a case. We asked him not to say anything to you until we were sure. If you'd like, I can be there with you when you tell him what happened today."

"Would you?" She shook her head and laughed. "Of course you would. You're such a good person. Such a good friend."

"I'd like to be more than a good friend, if you'd let me. After Connie died, I thought I'd never find love again until I met you. You've healed my heart. You're my best friend, the person I want to share everything with. I missed you so much when I was in D.C. You have no idea."

Grace smiled. "I feel the same way about you. My day is brighter every time you're around. And every time one of the guests does or says something funny, or Winston learns a new trick, you're the first person I want to share it with."

"Then we're on the same page," he said, his face lighting up with hope and happiness.

Grace gathered her words and strength. "I'm sorry, but we're not. Right now, I need some time to get over what just happened. Time to wrap my mind around everything that transpired."

"Are you still in love with Hank?" Spencer asked gently.

"No." She let the bittersweet tears fill her eyes without fighting them back. "The Hank Porter I loved disappeared a long time ago, because the man I loved would never have abandoned his family so casually. He wouldn't have turned his back on his son or swindled countless people. Or maybe I never really knew Hank. I'm not sure, and that's part of the problem."

Spencer stood and walked to the window, his back rigid, hands on his hips as he gazed at the lake. "You can't blame yourself for Hank's actions."

Grace walked over to Spencer and touched his shoulder, waiting to speak until he turned and met her eyes. "I'm not. I'm just tired and emotionally drained. The last thing I want is to lose you and your friendship. You deserve nothing but the best. Unfortunately, at the moment, I'm not at my best."

Spencer put his arms around Grace and pulled her close. He kissed the top of her head and whispered, "Be sure to take care of yourself. Take the time you need to heal. My friendship and I aren't going anywhere."

Hours later, as the sun set on Lake Haven with the sky painted in magnificent slashes of red, orange, and purple, Grace stood alone on the veranda and watched the lone egret. "It looks like it's just you and me tonight, Sola."

"And us."

Grace turned to find Charlotte standing behind her holding two covered plates on a tray along with three wineglasses. Winnie stood next to her with Winston in her arms.

"I thought you had a date with Dean," Grace said to her sister, then addressed her aunt. "And shouldn't you be home with Gus?"

"Dean's working tonight, so we had an early date," Charlotte explained. "He sent me home with dinner, and it smells divine. Besides, there was no way I'd leave you alone after the horrible day you had." She set the tray down and handed Grace and Winnie wineglasses.

"Charlotte called and told me everything." Winnie set Winston down and gave Grace a hug. "Your uncle kicked me out of the house and told me to take care of you."

"How are you holding up?" Charlotte asked.

Grace felt weak again, so she sat down. "I broke things off with Spencer for now."

Winston jumped onto her lap. Winnie sat in the chair next to Grace and took her hand, sympathy filling her eyes.

"Why did you do that?" Charlotte asked. "You and Spencer are great together."

"After what happened with Hank, I need some time to clear my head," Grace said. "Until I can put the past to rest, I can't move forward."

Her sister and aunt remained silent, but she could see the love, support, and understanding in their expressions. She was so blessed to have such a wonderful family and support system. Maybe in time, after her heart had healed once again from the loss, she'd be given a second chance with Spencer.

"I also called Jake." Tears welled up in her eyes again. Would they ever stop? "He took it better than I expected, and he still plans to come for a visit on Tuesday, so that will help. I also made an appointment with Pastor Abrams for tomorrow, and I took a nap."

"All good things. We'll get through this just like we've gotten through everything else in life—together," Winnie said.

With that one little statement, the loneliness that had been eating away at Grace's heart all afternoon started to slip way. She cuddled Winston. "I don't know what I'd do without all of you."

"Well, thankfully, you won't have to find out anytime soon," Charlotte said. "And despite the Hank situation, it was a good week. One full of second chances."

Grace smiled and raised her wineglass. "To second chances and to the family that gives them meaning."

Get your copy of the next book in the series, *Cherished Legacy*.

AVAILABLE NOW!

Can the Magnolia Harbor Inn's guests discover the courage to confront the past so they can embrace the future?